Midnight

JOHN RUSSO

Burning Bulb

PUBLISHING

Midnight
By **John Russo**

Burning Bulb Publishing
P.O. Box 4721
Bridgeport, WV 26330-4721
United States of America
www.BurningBulbPublishing.com

Cover designed by Melissa St. Giles.
Burning Bulb Publishing Edition.

Paperback Edition ISBN: 978-1-948278-34-8

Printed in the United States of America

For my mother and dad.

"Man is capable of perpetrating the worst barbarities imaginable in the name of holy science, holy religion, or holy truth."

—Morgan Drey, *The Appeal of Witchcraft*

PROLOGUE

From the dirt road, they heard the demon screaming in pain and rage. It was trapped! It was out in the field like the other one.

"Run. *Run!*" Mama cried. "Don't be afraid—I'm right behind you!" She hurried along on her thin legs, a stout club of birch wood in her hand. Luke and Abraham, ages fourteen and twelve, each had shovels. They were leading the way, running really fast.

Cynthia, at ten the youngest, could hardly keep up, but she had said the prayers, which had enticed the demon to their trap. She was thrilled and proud of herself and scared, too.

Behind her, Cyrus giggled. He was almost sixteen, but not smart. He huffed and puffed, trying to make his fat legs churn up distance.

The family scurried down off the shoulder of the dirt road and out into the weed-grown field where the creature was screaming.

They broke through a thicket of tall weeds and saw the thing in the middle of the gas company's right-of-way that cut a broad swath down the side of the mountain and across the field.

"It looks like Jimmy Peterson's, sister!" Abraham blurted.

But it wasn't of course. It was a demon.

"They can *look* like anything," Mama cautioned. "Don't dare get too close, Luke! Hit it with your shovel!" She stood back, brandishing her club.

The trapped thing wailed and screamed hideously. The steel jaws of the trap had bitten down hard, chomping clean through the white leg bone. There was plenty of blood. The thing couldn't get away because of the heavy steel chain and peg that had the trap anchored to the ground. Luke and Abraham always drove the pegs deep.

"*Hit* it!" Mama yelled encouragingly.

The demon stopped wailing momentarily and coward, looking surprisingly like Jimmy Peterson's little sister. Same reddish hair and freckles. But the eyes gave away the secret—they were a beast's green eyes, wild and flashing.

Luke stepped forward boldly and swung shovel with all his might with both hands. The demon had started screaming again, but it stopped. The edge of Luke's shovel blade had split open its face and skull.

"Hooray!" Abraham shouted as the demon reeled and thudded to the earth. He ran up and both he and Luke smashed up the thing with their shovels again and again. It sounded like beating a rug. Once in a while, the shovels hit each other making a loud clang. Luke and Abraham chopped at the creature's head, legs, and body. When they got done, it was a bloody mess. Its red hair was matted in blood.

"You did real good," Mama said afterward. "Now Cyrus could make a coffin and we'll have a funeral."

"Why did it look like Jimmy Peterson's sister," Cynthia asked, as Luke and Abraham stood back a few feet, breathing hard, looking down at their gruesome handiwork.

Mama got angry. "I *told* you they could take any form they want to—a rabbit or a possum, or even a human being. It's our job not to be taken in—if they're sent to us, we have to destroy them."

Cyrus borrowed Luke shovel and looking to mama for approval, hit the dead thing one more time on its shattered head.

CHAPTER 1

Nancy Johnson let the heavy door of the church swing shut behind her, dipped her fingers in holy water, and made a careful sign of the cross. She was seventeen, blonde, and pretty, and panicked over the thought of going to confession. For two years, she had lived in sin, committing mortal sins of the flesh with her boyfriend. Several months ago, she had broken up with him and the wounds of the breakup were beginning to heal, and she wanted to cleanse her soul. She had already vowed never to give in to another boy until she was married. She had done it out of love, but he had ditched her for someone else, leaving her to get over the agony and the shame.

Nancy was a small-town girl with a history of regular attendance at mass and frequent acceptance of the sacraments. She had graduated from the local parochial school, which only went up through eighth grade, then had enrolled in the public high school, but continued to take the required catechism lessons once a week in the basement of the church. She was not fanatically religious, but to the extent that she was, she felt she had fallen short of worthy ideals better lived up to by priests and nuns. She had a guilt complex. Her healthy sex drive often made her secretly wish for the day she could be married so her indulgence would no longer be considered sinful.

As she advanced down the aisle of the church with its high vaulted ceiling and looming crucifix, she felt humble, even intimidated. The place of worship had an aura of piety and holiness. The statues of Jesus, Mary, and Joseph were shrouded in purple for the Lenten season and would be unveiled on Easter Sunday to celebrate the rising of Christ from the dead.

A few old ladies in black dresses and babushkas knelt in the pews. Not many people came to confession on hot Sunday afternoons. Nancy had been banking on this because she didn't want to stand in line. She wanted to get the ordeal over with before she lost her nerve.

During the past two years, she had gone to confession ten times without telling the priest she was having carnal relations with her boyfriend. And each of the ten times she had taken communion at mass the following day, accepting the sacraments while not in a state of grace, which was the most horrible mortal sin a person could commit: sacrilege. She had been afraid to tell the priest she had given into sex. And she had gone to the rail for communion, anyway, because her mother always went to mass with her and would have known something was funny if her daughter stopped taking the sacrament.

Nancy genuflected, squeezed between two pews, and lowered a padded kneeler to the floors as her knees bent to meet it. She prayed, reading from the chapter on preparation for confession in her missile. Oh, my God! Cracked me like to be truly sorry for my sins. To think that I have offended thee after being forgiven so many times I lay the rest of my life at the feet that it atone for my past. Mary, mother of God, help me to make a good confession. Leaving the pew, she entered the confessional and shut the door softly. Her knees found the kneeler in the dark. There was a cloth covered aperture through which the priest on the other side of the compartment would be able to hear her voice as she hoped he would not recognize it. Father Flaherty had said in cataclysm class that God helped him and all the other priests never to remember a confession or a confessor. But Nancy did not lean too close to the aperture for fear he could see through it.

"Bless me, Father, for I have sinned. It is two years since my last good confession." Father Flaherty's voice came back so loudly that Nancy just knew everybody in the church could hear.

"Speak up! I can't hear you. Come closer to the screen."

She inched closer, than repeated herself.

"You say it's been *two years* since your last good confession?" Father's voice was shocked. Incredulous.

"Yes, father." Nancy meekly admitted her throat was dry, her tongue thick, her voice low and horse. She perspired profusely.

"Let me get this straight, young lady. Do you mean to tell me that during the past two years you just haven't been to confession? Or do you mean that you made bad confessions during this time??

"I made bad confessions, Father."

There was a lengthy silence that Nancy was sure the priest needed to recover from being stunned.

Then, "These bad conventions—how many did you say?"

"Ten, Father."

"How do you mean they were bad? Did you fail to tell some senior were guilty of?"

"Yes, Father."

"And why in the world did you do that?"

"I don't know. I was afraid."

"What sin were you afraid to tell?"

"Having carnal relations with my boyfriend, Father."

"I see. Is he Catholic?"

"He was, Father. But we broke up."

"It was undoubtedly the best thing that could have happened. You were living in sin with him, do you realize that?"

"Yes, Father."

"And yet you failed to tell these mortal sins in confession so you might receive forgiveness. Does that make good sense to you? You realize surely that this kind of sin is grievous enough to send you into eternal damnation?"

"Yes, Father."

"Would you rather go to Hell for all eternity than suffer a bit of embarrassment here in the confessional?"

"No, Father."

"All right." Father Stephen sucked in his breath and delivered the question Nancy dreaded most. "Did you afterward go to communion with these mortal sins on your soul?"

"Yes. I'm sorry, Father."

"Oh, my gosh! Do you mean to tell me that you existed in a state of mortal sin for two years? That during this time you defiled the sacrament ten times just because you were ashamed to confess your sins."

"Yes, Father."

The priest let out a long sigh of exasperation.

"You have committed the grievous sin of sacrilege ten times by making false confessions. And you have each time committed the worst sacrilege of accepting our Lord's body and blood while in the state of mortal sin. This is one of the most awful sins a Catholic can commit. Do you realize that you can burn in Hell forever for this one sin? Do you understand that for a period of two years, the power of sanctifying grace was absent from your soul? If you had died at any time during these two years, you would right at this instance be burning in Hell. Your immortal soul would have descended directly into the arms of Satan!"

"I know, Father, and I'm sorry."

"What other sins have you committed? Go on with your confession and make it a good one, young lady."

Telling the rest of it was almost easy compared with the magnitude of what Nancy had just been through. She finally said, "That is all, Father."

The priest replied, "Now make a good act of contrition and for your penance say ten rosaries. Ask Jesus to help you avoid temptation and come to mass and make good confessions and take communion more often."

"I will. Father." Nancy could hear the priest praying in Latin behind the screen while she said her act of contrition in English.

"Oh my God, I am heartily sorry for having offended thee and I detest all my sins because I dread the loss of heaven and the pains of hell. But most of all, because I have offended thee, My God, who art all good and deserving of all my love. I firmly resolve with the help of thy grace, to confess my sins, to do penance and to amend my life. Amen."

She waited for Father Stephen's Latin to come to an end so she could receive her final blessing. "In the name of the Father and the Son and the Holy Spirit, Amen. May God bless you."

"Thank you, father."

Still smarting from embarrassment, Nancy stepped out of the church into gusting spring air that soon evaporated the perspiration on her brow. She began to feel greatly relieved as she raised her arms over her head to let the breeze dry and cool her underarms. Across the street from the church. She cut through a grassy field on her way home. The sunlight felt good, and she enjoyed the blue sky and the freshness all around her, and she knew it had been a long time since she had felt so happy and clean.

She looked at her watch, ten minutes to one. Her stepfather ought to be home by the time she got there, and he had promised to let her use his car to go shopping.

A local policeman, Bert Johnson, was off duty at noon on Saturdays, but he usually would stop for a few drinks after work. Nancy decided that if he wasn't home yet, she'd take a shower, wash and dry her hair and call up her girlfriend, Patty. Maybe Patty would want to go to the mall too.

As she walked, her stride unusually light and carefree, Nancy began saying her rosaries.

CHAPTER 2

Bert Johnson, Nancy's stepfather, drank by himself at the long, dimly lit bar. The only other customers in the place where two drunks playing the bowling machine, the old-fashioned kind with balls instead of pucks. Bert was so wound up in his own thoughts that the drunks' curses, niggling arguments and braying, booze-thickened laughter do not bother him. Neither did the rolling thunder of their bowling. Bert was nursing his fifth double bourbon and draft chaser.

An outburst of exceptional raucousness caught his attention and, half turning, he saw out of the corner of his eye that the one drunk had sneaked up behind his buddy, who was in the act of launching a ball and pulled his pants down. The ball went ricocheting and down the gutter as the bowler, to stupefied to react, straightened up, slowly muttering to himself, his stained and tattered underwear and fat fish belly white buttocks quivering in the fluorescence of the bowling machine.

"Hey!" Sleepy the bartender yelled. "Don't you two clowns know there's a *policeman* in here? You want to get busted for indecent exposure?"

"What's so all-fire indecent about it?" the drunk pulling his pants up slurred indignantly. "My ass is as decent as *you* ever seen. I ain't got nothin' I aint proud of."

"How do you like *that*?" Sleepy said to Bert. "Why is it most of my customers are refugees from the loony farm?"

Bert didn't answer. Instead, he drained his shot and chaser. This was his way of letting Sleepy know he didn't want conversation. Taking the hint, the bartender refilled the bourbon and the beer and moved on down to the far end of the bar to keep a close eye on the bowlers.

Sleepy kept a baseball bat under the set of shelves near where he stood and was fully prepared to charge out and use it if it looked like the two drunks were going to get rambunctious enough to maybe break something.

Bert Johnson, contemplating his reflection in the mirror behind the bar, ran his thick, stubby fingers through his thinning brown hair. His policeman's cap was parked on the bar stool beside him. The weight of his service revolver and nightstick pulled down on his gun belt, making his poncho uncomfortable. He hitched up his belt in trousers, lifting his wide rear end off the stool a few inches till this maneuver was accomplished.

He averted his eyes from the mirror because his appearance disturbed him. He was no longer young, no longer decent looking, no longer in good physical condition. His nose, always a trifle large for his face, now had some broken capillaries from drinking too much. He was well aware that he ought to cut down, but he could not find the incentive to do so.

He was disgusted with his marriage. His wife, Harriet, almost youthfully attractive and desirable when he married her six years ago, had immediately started showing her age and put on 30 or 40 pounds. Bert felt that she had somehow cheated him, by not obliging herself to remain sexually appealing. He would not have married her in the first place if he had known he could not continue to be proud of her appearance and stimulated by her.

Not that sex was everything; but more and more, a saying Bert had heard once seemed to be true, that when a marriage went bad, it went bad in bed. Did Harriet love him or not? He wasn't sure. Maybe all she ever really cared about was trapping a man. Someone to take care of her and her daughter so she could relax and let herself go to pot.

Bert liked to think he was still young, only forty-five, plenty of life in him. Yet for the right woman, a woman who could make him feel like taking care of himself again. Still in all, he didn't want a divorce. In fact, he was rather frightened of the prospect. He didn't want Harriet to leave him. He had been lonely and sexually frustrated through most of the years, preceding his courtship with her

Up to age thirty-nine, he had never been married, had not dated much, had never felt really free to make a life for himself till his father passed away, crippled by a steel mill accident. The old man had needed him badly. And how could Bert have expected any woman he might have married to accept a 70-year-old invalid as part of the package?

So, Bert had waited, devoting himself to be in a good, hardworking cop and watching the good things in life passing by. His marriage to Harriet seemed like a fresh beginning, almost too good to be true. The status of married man pleased Bert, even though it was starting to go sour. He had been much less happy before. If only Harriet, it would do something about herself!

In his stepdaughter, Nancy, Bert could see the youth in sensuality that once had belonged to Harriet. Sometimes his eyes stayed on her too long when she paraded through the house wearing a skimpy pair of shorts and a flimsy T shirt with no bra. Maybe she did it to tease him. He didn't think so, but he wasn't sure. He had to remind himself to look upon her as his daughter, not as a sexy young girl. He was ashamed to admit even to himself that he sometimes felt these unmentionable stirrings toward her.

With a tingle of excitement in his groin, Bert mulled over an instant that happened last night while he was on duty. An anonymous caller had phoned police headquarters to report a car parked behind the high school, and Bert's squad car had been dispatched to check out a possible attempted vandalism or breaking and entering.

"Probably just a couple of teenagers screwing," Al McCoy, Bert's partner, had said.

But still they had to be careful and take the usual precautions.

And so, driving slowly up the road to where the school was, Bert killed the headlights and pulled the car off the shoulder, and he and Al got out. They proceeded on foot, flashlights ready and weapons drawn, knowing they had a good chance of catching the perpetrators red handed.

Thinking about it now, Bert was almost ready to admit to himself that both he and Al

probably secretly wanted to catch some pretty young thing with her pants down. When they got up close to the target vehicle, a late-model Chevy with the front windows wound down on a warm evening, they could see the chasse rocking and could hear the undeniable sounds of lovemaking coming from inside. Bert didn't know why he and Al didn't simply holster their service revolvers and slink on out of there, leaving the kids alone. They obviously weren't trying to break into the school. They already had what they had come for.

As if under some kind of compulsion, Bert now sneaked up on the car till Al was looking in on the passenger side, Bert on the driver's side. For a long time, they both just stood watching... the nakedly entwined bodies clearly illuminated by moonlight, totally unaware that they were no longer alone. All at once, as if on signal, Al and Bert turned on their flashlights. The boy jumped and hollered. immediately losing his erection. As he turned over, the girl screamed. She was a good looker, with long black hair and large firm breasts, no more than fifteen or sixteen years old.

The boy scrambled for his clothes, got a piece of her red slacks over his groin. But she couldn't grab hold of anything and tried to hide her body behind his. She had stopped screaming and just starcd wide eyed as a frightened doe, and Bert couldn't take his eyes off the nipple that wasn't hidden behind the boy's naked back.

"Cops!" the boy scoffed, an attempt at bravado. "What in the hell do you want?"

He was older than the girl, maybe in his early twenties, and was making a show of regaining his cool. He even had the gall to start pulling his pants on, the flashlights helping him to see what he was doing, but also putting pretty good illumination on his girlfriend.

"Billie! For God's sake!" she blurted because his body was no longer protecting hers from view.

Al and Bert kept ogling her.

"We weren't doing anything wrong. You have to let us go." the boy in the car said.

"Cool as a cucumber ain't you?" Al drawled sarcastically. "You ever heard of corrupting the morals of a minor? I ought a smack you one in the teeth with his flashlight, teach you to mind who you're talking to."

"Get dressed—*both* of you!" Bert snapped. His mouth was dry, and he was nervous. Ashamed of himself, he realized he had the beginning of an erection. He kept his light trained on the occupants of the car, ostensibly so they could find their clothes. The girls breast hung ripe and full when she bent to pick up her blouse, and Bert saw how good her thighs were as she slithered into her panties and slacks.

When the two were dressed, Al kept his flashlight on them while he delivered a stern lecture about how the girl was obviously a minor, and what would her parents do if she and her boyfriend got booked for disporting themselves lewdly in a public place? Not to mention a possible jail sentence for the boy for corrupting the morals of a minor. She started to cry while he remained morosely silent, conveying the impression that he was not repentant but dragged.

Bert kept thinking about the girl's body.

"We could have screwed her." Al said as the young couple drove off.

Bert turned the key in the ignition of squad car.

We could have *had* her," Al insisted, "if we wasn't such square honest cops. We would have got some for not turnin' her in."

Annoyed, Bert said, "Her boyfriend never would've stood still for a shakedown like that.

"You think not? What's *he* care. It's no skin off his ass. I didn't get the idea he was in love with her, know what I mean?

"Let's drop it, huh?"

"Okay, okay!" Al replied testily. "I'm just saying we passed up a good opportunity to get laid."

"She had a fine body," Bert admitted wistfully.

"Damn right," Al said. I could stand a shot at something young and fine. Doing it with my fat old lady is about as much fun as shoving it into a cud-chewing, complacent cow."

Bert thought of Harriet… and Nancy.

CHAPTER 3

Sliding her hand along the smooth, curved mahogany railing, Cynthia mounted the stairs to her Mama's room. She knocked and entered. As usual. Mama was in her rocking chair.

"It's getting on toward Easter," Cynthia said. "Time for our congregation to be gathering. There'll be almost two hundred of them this time—some from as far away as California."

Mama never spoke much anymore, but Cynthia could read her thoughts and knew she was pleased. So many people coming to the services!

Cynthia told her Mama, "Luke and Abraham have the chapel all spic and span. Cyrus is making coffins. Some of the people who've been here for services before will bring food and do the cooking. Don't you fret. You don't have to do any of the hard work. We'll do it like you taught us."

But Mama seemed worried, so to cheer her up, Cynthia said, "We'll have three young girls for the midnight rituals. Luke and Abraham already have one captured. We'll get two more by Easter Sunday."

This seemed to gladden Mama some. "Wish Papa could be here," Cynthia almost told her, but she refrained from mentioning it out loud. Instead, she smiled and said, "Lots of interesting people going be here for the services.

Cynthia still missed Papa occasionally, but Mama didn't like to talk about him anymore, since ten years ago when he ran away.

"Everything is right on schedule, Mama," Cynthia said. "No cause for you to worry."

CHAPTER 4

In bra and panties, Nancy Johnson sat cross-legged on her bed, talking with a girlfriend, Patty, over the cell phone. She had taken her shower and was now brushing her hair, cradling the phone between shoulder and chin to leave her hands free. It did not bother her that her radio was blaring rock music from a Top 40 station. She liked being home alone so she could do these sort of things without being yelled at. Her mother would have told her to turn off the radio or hang up the phone, one of the other, if she didn't want to go into adulthood wearing hearing aid. Patty had just confided a certain boy she was interested in had finally asked her prom.

"He *did*? Oh, I'm so happy for you! I told you he'd get up the nerve eventually. I saw the way he kept staring at you in homeroom. He's really *shy*. I bet the two you will hit it off."

"But I'm the opposite of shy," Patty protested, obviously considering shyness and undesirable quality.

"I know," said Nancy, "your outgoing personality is the perfect balance for Bob's shyness. Don't you know what I mean? opposites attract."

"Yeah, I guess so," Patti said, perking up.

Nancy had got done brushing her hair and was appraising her body in the mirror, turned this way and that, wondering if her breasts were large enough and whether her legs were too thin. Meantime, Patty was explaining that she was sorry she'd have to pass up the shopping trip to the mall because her mother, it outlined a program of chores. "On Saturday too!" Patty lamented.

Just then, Nancy's doorbell rang.

"Hang on a minute, Patty, I think I hear my stepfather at the door."

Laying the telephone receiver down on the bed. Nancy tugged on her nightgown and went to the front door—as the bell rang again and again, insistently. When she flung the door wide open Bert Johnson was out on the porch, leering at her, and grabbing onto the door frame so he wouldn't fall down.

Nancy stepped back, frowning, seeing immediately that he was drunk, giving him room to enter without staggering into her.

"Hello, Daddy," she said.

In a brazen and slurring voice, Bert Johnson blurted. "*Good* morning, sweetheart How about a big smooch for your old man, huh?

Nancy stared at him. H e had often been drunk in her presence, but this business about a smooch was definitely out of character. Her stepfather had always maintained an almost cold aloofness toward her, not ever really taking the place of her real father. So this sudden change in him was alarming, although Nancy didn't specifically know why. But she knew enough to begin to get scared.

Lunging forward, he stumbled into her and hung onto her shoulders to support himself, pressing her against the wall.

"Daddy!" she gasped, getting a face full of the liquor on his breath.

He pushed himself away from her, keeping her trapped between his two extended arms. His voice was low, husky, almost pleading. "You don't need to call me and Daddy all the time, Nancy. I'm only your stepfather, and we both know it. There's a no blood between us. So there's nothin' wrong with being nice to me once in a while. "How 'bout a little kiss, huh?"

Bert perked up, suddenly looking around listening. "Where is your mother?" he whispered warily.

Ducking under his arms, Nancy backed away from him toward her room. "She went to the beauty parlor to get her hair done. Remember, she said I could use your car today to go shopping, can I?" With these questions, she hoped to divert his attention away from her.

She trembled, seeing a gleam in his eyes which she did not like.

Tossing his policeman's cap onto a seat in the hallway, he lunged at her, grabbing her by the wrist and pulling her to him in a drunken embrace. "Sure, I'll give you the car, honey. Now, where's my big hug and kiss? How's about it, huh? I won't bite you."

She averted her face and he kissed her wetly on the cheek. She was afraid to push him away, for she sensed that outright rejection might make in turn angry and violent. Maybe she could talk her way out of this.

"Daddy, you're hurting me. Please let me go. My girlfriend Patty is on the phone. She's waiting for me to get back on the line. I told her you were ringing the doorbell."

He loosened his grip and she squirmed away from him and hastened into her bedroom, shutting the door. She took a deep breath, pulling herself together. Then she picked up the telephone which had been left lying on the bed.

"Patty, I'm back. Patty? Are you there? Ooh—darn it! Why'd she have to hang up?"

Bert Johnson slumped under the settee in the hall a few feet from Nancy's bedroom. He felt guilty and ashamed and erotically aroused all at the same time. The worst thing for him would be if his passing a stepdaughter went nowhere. She could hold it over him, maybe even tell her mother. And Harriet would divorce him. Damn it. That little tease! She had been flaunting herself at him, and walking around the house so provocatively all the time—and now that she had goaded him into making his move, she pretended to be scared. What she want—to be coaxed?

When Nancy cradled the phone, she looked anxiously toward her closed bedroom door. As she got up with the idea of sliding the bolt shut, the door banged open, making her jump back, and her stepfather entered, gazing at her boldly. He had removed his shirt and was now naked to the waist, his fat belly hanging over his wide black policeman's belt.

"Come here, now, Nancy, honey…show Bert some of the lovin' he don't get from your mother."

"Daddy, leave me alone!" Nancy backed away thinking maybe she should have stood her ground. Perhaps a show of strength and determination would have controlled him. But she wasn't thinking clearly at all.

"Just let me look at you." He pleaded. "I won't lay a hand on your body, I promise. Take your nightgown off for me. Let me see what you *really* look like. We don't need to go any further than just looking…unless you want to."

"But…you can't be in your right mind. You don't know what you're saying. You're my *stepfather*! Get out of my room right now! Or I'll tell my mother when she comes home."

"Come on, now…I know you have to put up a show of resistance to keep yourself respect. But you can't tell me you're a virgin. I heard you and your boyfriend one night out on the porch."

"Get out of my *room*!"

Nancy cowered as he lurched for her, his hands reaching for her breasts. She managed to sidestep him at the last instant and slapped him in the face with all her might. He stopped in his tracks, glaring at her, breathing hoarsely with sudden savage movement. He ripped at her tearing open her nightgown. She started sobbing as he seized her shoulders and spun her around, roughly stripping the flimsy garment offer and flinging her to the floor.

She couldn't believe this was happening. She stood there, crying while he ogled her near nakedness.

He got her in a bear hug, pressing his heavy, drunken kisses upon her. He fumbled at her bra and because he could not hold her so tightly while he was thus occupied, she struggled and squirmed, almost managing to get loose, but his knee shoved into her between her legs. He used his superior strength of push her down onto the bed. She tried to kick and squirm, but his massive weight bore down on her, taken her breath away. Straddling her, he got his thick hands on her breasts. His right hand moved downward, caressing her torso and hips as he worked her panties down off her legs.

He was so caught up in what he was doing, he failed to stop Nancy from getting her hands on the portable radio line behind her on the pillow, still blasting rock music

Clutching the radio, she swung it as hard as she could down on the top of her stepfather's balding head. He grunted in pain and surprise. Then his face sagged as he collapsed, unconscious.

Disheveled and scared out of her wits, Nancy extricated herself from beneath him. She, pulled up her panties and, glimpsing her bare breasts in the mirror, hastily snatched her bra off the floor and put it back on.

For a moment, she was afraid she might have killed her stepfather with the blow on the head, so she picked up his arm, felt for the pulse in his wrist, then let the arm drop. His knuckles smacked the floor and his arm dangled over the edge of the bed. He began to snore. Nancy, look down on him, disbelievingly, full of anxiety mixed with relief.

What would he be like when he came to? How would Nancy and her mother and he ever go on living together in the same house?

Backing around the bed, she went to her closet, rummaged, and pulled out a suitcase. Pushing bottles of makeup in her large jewelry box out of the way, she made room for the suitcase on top of her dresser, then began opening drawers and going through them, filling the suitcase with clothes and other belongings.

Bert Johnson, lying flat on his back, continued to snore loudly.

Nancy felt frightened, worried, alone—shut out, rudely and suddenly from a world she had believed be reasonably comfortable, loving and safe. She knew she had to leave home. But she had no clear idea of where to run.

CHAPTER 5

Cynthia remembered when they first started using the traps. From the time she first saw them, she was fascinated with their gadgetry, although they did not belong to her but to her brothers, Luke and Abraham. Cyrus, her oldest brother, was too addlebrained to be allowed to play with anything so dangerous. For some reason, though, he was very good at making little wooden coffins to bury birds and mice. Luke and Abraham had three traps each, given to them by Uncle Sal.

Cynthia recalled the serrated steel set with a strong hook and spring, the Fiat metal lever where the bait was put, and the steel chain and peg that kept the trap anchored. It started before the traps, though, really. It started with Mama and the things she taught Cynthia and her brothers from the time they were babies, when the whole family lived up above the shop where Mama sold magical herbs, potions, amulets, and books to strange people who came from as far away as New York and Philadelphia. Papa was still with the family then and took them all to visit Uncle Sal and Aunt Edna on holidays.

Cynthia sat with her legs tucked under her in the back seat of the car. She had on a pink starched dress, her shiny black hair combed and brushed. She could see the back of Papa's head and tried to imagine the thoughts that were going on there. She could see the left side of Mama's rouged face and part of her left shoulder. If she stood up on the car seat, and Mama didn't catch her, she could see more, could glue her eyes to the snaky, white unraveling road line or watch white guardposts rushing by in endless cable-linked procession until her eyes got sore and she had to sit down before Mama yelled at her.

"You stay in your seat, Cynthia! If we hit a hard bump or Papa has to make a quick stop, you'll go flying right out the window."

Such a thing seemed unlikely, especially with the window closed. But Mama must be right. Or why would people come from so far away to have her cell the magic things or read their fortunes?

Cynthia and her three brothers, crammed together in the back seat of the sedan, looked at each other and giggled. Luke, all pink-cheeked and polished with his yellow hair plastered down, had on a sailor outfit with long pants and a real starched-white sailor's cap. Abraham was wearing a soldier suit with short pants, which made him mad when Papa bought it for him. He had never seen a soldier with short pants but he felt better when Papa showed him the hat that came with the outfit, a realistic officer's cap with a shiny black beak and imitation gold braid. Cyrus was big and chubby for his age, and he was wearing green trousers like the kind bus drivers wear, a white short-sleeved shirt, and gray suspenders, and he dressed that way most of the time and looked kind of funny because Mama could never find regular clothes to fit him.

Cynthia thought of her Easter basket, which Mama had made her leave at home. "You're not gonna spoil your appetite, young lady. Aunt Edna and Uncle Sal will have plenty of sweet stuff for you." Luke and Abraham had to leave their baskets home too. But Cyrus was allowed to bring his with him, which was a laugh because his candy was nearly all gone. The pink, crinkly straw was a mess, stained with melted chocolate and jellybeans. Cyrus had saved a few of the yellow marshmallow rabbits to eat last because he liked them best, as did Cynthia. Real gooey and soft, they stretched and snapped apart between your teeth, then melted like powdered sugar on your tongue.

"The Easter celebration originally had nothing whatsoever to do with Jesus," Mama had said. "It was a pagan rite of spring. Rabbits and eggs are symbols of fertility, of giving birth, thus, the Easter bunny delivering eggs. Understand, children?"

Cynthia didn't, not when she was seven years old. Maybe Luke and Abraham understood more. To Cyrus, it meant absolutely nothing. All he understood about Easter was biting the head off a marshmallow rabbit.

When they had been piling into the car, some of their school friends had been starting off for church. "Why don't we go to church?" Cynthia had asked.

"Because we don't believe in it," Mama had replied. "We believe in things that are much older than the church, and a great deal more powerful. Church is for weaklings. It's not for us, as it wasn't for your grandfather or great-grandfather either."

"*Tell* us about Grandpa," Luke begged at one point during the long car ride.

"Well, he was a Cunning Man," Mama began, "as was his father, before him."

"What's *that*?" Cynthia piped up, though they had all heard the explanation many times before.

"A Cunning Man is a witch doctor," Mama explained. "The word 'cunning' means wise, sly, crafty. So Grandpa Barnes was a wise man. In the village where he lived in England, he was known as a magician. He could do wonderful and sometimes very frightening things that made the people's hair stand on end. He was feared and respected. But he had followers, his own congregation, so to speak. His magic wasn't the fake kind that you see on television, it was real. It came from his knowledge of demons."

"Where are they?" one of the children asked.

"They live in hell," Mama said. "They work for Satan or for whoever knows how to summon them with magic."

"Did Grandpa know how?"

"The people said he did. They said he could make people die by compelling them to do so."

Cynthia didn't understand "compelling," but it sounded horrible.

"You shouldn't fill the kids' minds with this kind of stuff," Papa interjected.

"But it's all true," Mama insisted. "Besides, it's no worse than the Hansel and Gretel stories; people getting pushed into ovens and all."

"I disagree," Papa stated flatly.

To show him that she would talk about whatever she wanted to, Mama stubbornly told still more stories about Grandpa Luke Barnes and his father, Abraham Barnes, both Cunning Men, for whom Cynthia's brothers, Luke and Abraham were named. The Cunning Men could, according to Mama, fly through the air under their own power and could pass invisibly through walls. They knew how to foretell the future, locate buried or stolen treasure, and cure sick people or animals merely by touching them and reciting magical spells.

Cynthia and her brothers listened with solemn, rapt attention to these awesome stories. Many of them they had heard before, but they always enjoyed having them repeated. They particularly liked hearing Mama tell about Grandpa Barnes' battle with a witch from a neighboring village in England. This old woman had caused Grandpa to come down with a severe case of arthritis. With the aid of certain ancient charms and talismans known only to him, Grandpa consulted his magic mirror. The identity of the enemy witch was revealed in the mirror and Grandpa knew what to do. He followed her home one night over a dark path in the woods and carefully stabbed each of her footprints with a brand- new knife over which he had recited a special prayer to a demon. The demon made the witch fall dead on her own threshold and Grandpa's arthritis was cured.

"Poppycock!" Papa scoffed. He was wearing his gray sharkskin suit with the peppermint necktie. He smelled like aftershave lotion, the kind he had once dabbed on Cynthia's face to let her feel how much it burned. His stiffly starched white shirt collar had rubbed the back of his neck red and his hair was edged in the neat arc of a fresh haircut around his ears. White skin showed in places through his thinning black hair. Cynthia found herself noticing everything about him because he was home so seldom. Most of the time he was away on long business trips, and then he would show up finally with presents, like the pink dress for Cynthia, Abraham's and Luke's soldier and sailor suits, and Mama's earrings.

"Sheldon, don't you dare make fun of my ancestors," Mama said. "I believe firmly that their spirits are with us, protecting this family."

"You don't believe in religion but you believe in that nonsense," Papa grumped. "Don't blame me if the children grow up to be a pack of superstitious fools. Why don't you save the spiel for your customers? It's all right in its proper place when you're making a buck out of it."

Mama did not deign to reply to this but her silent anger permeated the closed-in car. She had ordered all the windows to be kept tightly wound shut so the wind wouldn't mess up her new permanent. Only a finger-thick crack was allowed in Cyrus' window so he wouldn't get carsick. Mama looked nice wearing the navy-blue suit Papa had bought her for her birthday. Her lips were red, her cheeks rosy; not pale like when she talked to customers or ironed clothes. Cynthia could see one of her white earrings and her pearl necklace fastened with a tiny hook and chain behind her neck, and the big white Easter flower almost hidden by her shoulder. Her perfume, like the flower, smelled sticky-sweet in the hot, stuffy car.

"Children, listen to me," she said when her anger subsided, "don't forget to wish Aunt Edna and Uncle Sal a happy Easter. They'll have some presents for you, I'm sure. You must remember to say thank you. We taught you some manners, don't be afraid to use them. You too, Cyrus."

Papa parked the car in Uncle Sal's long gravel driveway and the whole family got out; Mama helping Cyrus with his Easter basket. Looking up at the house, a large and stately building of red brick with a wide veranda and tall white pillars in front, Cynthia was awed and impressed by it, as usual. It was a real Southern mansion. According to Uncle Sal, the man who owned this place prior to the Civil War also owned slaves. Then later, he became the overseer and landlord of all the sharecroppers and tenant farmers in the valley.

Most of the farms were inactive now, although people still lived 'round about, sometimes putting in small gardens for their own use, but mostly earning a living from the nearby coal mines. Uncle Sal wasn't a farmer or a miner. He was an artist who had come here for peace and quiet. There was an old country church on his property, a hundred yards or so from the house, which had once been the Sunday come-to-meeting place for all the farmers in the valley who worked, played and prayed under the wing of their overseer. Now the hundred-year-old church was Uncle Sal's studio, where he churned out oil paintings of the good old days to be sold to art galleries, department stores, and other customers on commission.

Cynthia loved to go into the church to look at Uncle Sal's work and she hoped she would be allowed to later, but they always had to go to the house to eat first. She noticed how the gravel stones scampered away as she walked on them or else bounced up and put marks on her white Easter shoes. Mama grabbed her hand and pulled her along angrily, as if it was her fault, while Cyrus waddled in front without a care in the world, swinging his Easter basket. Luke and Abraham, in their soldier and sailor outfits, walked smartly behind Papa, stiffly aware that they were members of the military. Papa rapped his knuckles on the screen door and without waiting to be admitted, led the way through the living room and into the steamy, good-smelling kitchen.

Aunt Edna came running excitedly from the dining room. "Happy Easter!" she shrieked, letting out a big, silly laugh and pushing her eyeglasses back up the bridge of her nose. Her white apron was stained with gravy and cherry juice. Cynthia and the boys immediately began thinking of cherry pie while Mama and Aunt Edna hugged and kissed like they always did on holidays. Uncle Sal had followed behind Edna to shake hands with Papa.

"Let the two sisters smooch each other for a while," he said in his gruff manner, smiling. "Want a shot of bourbon, Shelly?"

Papa said, "No, not right now, Sal. Happy Easter. I'll take a beer, though, if you have one."

"Happy Easter, Cindy! What did the Easter Bunny bring you?" Stooping over, Aunt Edna hugged Cynthia so hard it hurt, then turned her loose with a big "Um" and planted a rough, watery kiss on her cheek. Then she did the same to the boys, which embarrassed them, except for Cyrus, who didn't know any better. The kiss made Cynthia's cheek cold and wet but she was ashamed to let her aunt see her wipe it off so she simply waited for it to dry.

Uncle Sal shook hands with all the boys. To Cyrus, he said, "That's a real good-looking basket you have there kid but the candy's all gone. You're a regular sweet tooth."

Cyrus held the basket out, so Sal bent over, pretended to select and eat a jelly bean. "Oh, boy, that was good!" Uncle Sal growled, rubbing his stomach and grinning to make Cyrus feel good.

Uncle Sal was a small, trim man with a ragged brown mustache. Around the house, he always wore a pair of the paint-daubed blue jeans that he wore in the studio. His manner was gruff, cheerful, and informal, and the children liked him.

"I have some special goodies for you kids," beamed Aunt Edna. "I'll show them to you now but you have to promise not to touch them till after supper so you won't spoil your appetites. Do I have your word of honor?"

"Yes, Aunt Edna! We promise!"

"Cross your hearts."

They did so, getting fun out of it.

"Okay," said Aunt Edna. "You're gonna have a real surprise."

"Yeah, kids," said Uncle Sal, laughing. "We have some pregnant rabbits for you."

"Sal!" Aunt Edna chided. "Watch how you talk around the children."

"Nothing wrong with being pregnant," Sal countered. "How do you think they came into the world in the first place?"

Mama said, "It's all right, Sal. I didn't raise them to be frightened of sex."

"Yeah, but you're scaring them silly with your crazy witch stories," Papa complained, pouring beer into a glass.

Mama glowered at him but he didn't seem to notice.

Aunt Edna had turned to the kitchen cabinet and opened the doors so she could reach to the highest shelf. She brought out a large flat tray and held it so Cynthia and the boys could have a look. The tray contained four gingerbread bunnies with white button eyes and frosted whiskers, and each bunny had a hard-boiled egg for a stomach. The children eyed their pregnant rabbits with amusement then squinted at each other and laughed and giggled.

"Thank you, Aunt Edna! Thank you, Uncle Sal!"

Cyrus was the only one who forgot to say thank you. His mouth hanging open, he kept ogling the pregnant rabbits as if he half-expected them to get up and run away.

"I don't want any thanks, kids!" Uncle Sal exclaimed. "I don't do any of the baking around here; I just bring home the dough." He winked and all the adults laughed but the children didn't get it.

Aunt Edna's holiday meal was lavish and delicious. As on all holidays and special occasions, each of the children was permitted to have a shot glass of home-made wine as an appetizer. Cynthia sipped hers cautiously, but, even so, her eyes watered and her throat burned. But she continued to sip it a little at a time till she got sort of used to it. And when it was gone her cheeks glowed and her belly felt warm and good. Luke and Abraham were able to drink theirs faster, almost like grown-ups. Then Aunt Edna served mashed potatoes and gravy and thick slabs of juicy turkey; pickles, celery, olives, and radishes; hot buttered cornbread, green beans, coleslaw, and root beer. And the grand finale; cherry pie topped with vanilla ice cream.

Cynthia and her brothers, all sitting on one side of the large dining table, leaned back and compared bellies. "Look at all of you," said Uncle Sal. "Swelled up like four little basketballs. I think I'll take you outside and dribble you. You first, Cynthia."

"I bet you couldn't dribble Cyrus," Cynthia said. The grown-ups thought this was cute and got a laugh out of it. Cyrus smiled lopsidedly, aware somehow that he had become an object of attention.

"This one's gonna be the brains of the family," Uncle Sal pronounced, meaning Cynthia, and she glowed inwardly, embarrassed yet pleased by the compliment.

"Now, Uncle Sal and I have got more surprises for you," announced Aunt Edna. She trotted up the stairs and stayed away for a few minutes, which seemed to Cynthia and the boys like an excruciatingly long time.

But at last her high heels clicked into the room and she was laden with packages, one for each child.

Cyrus opened his first and his present turned out to be a big toy shovel with a long wooden handle and shiny steel blade; a good shovel, one you could actually dig with, not one that would bend or break easily. Cyrus smiled his lopsided smile.

The boxes given to Abraham and Luke were quite large and when opened were found to contain three steel traps for each boy, given to them by Uncle Sal who had not forgotten his last year's promise to teach them how to set bait and trap wild animals like rabbits, raccoons, and possums. "Maybe you'll even catch the Easter Bunny, who knows?"

Cynthia laughed. Luke and Abraham were thrilled even though at first they may have been a trifle disappointed that they were considered too young to be given BB guns. Luke was ten and Abraham was eight.

Cynthia opened her package and found a shovel just like Cyrus'. She liked to get toys instead of dresses all the time and loved her Aunt Edna and Uncle Sal for understanding this. Immediately, her head was filled with visions of using her new shovel to dig a pirate cave such as the one she had seen in her first- grade reading book. Or better yet, if Mama would teach her some magic, maybe she could find some buried treasure like Grandpa Barnes, the Cunning Man.

"Is there such a thing as a Cunning Girl?" Cynthia asked. "Because I'd like to be one when I grow up."

Everybody laughed except Papa.

"It would be called a Cunning Woman," Mama told Cynthia. "And you can't just simply decide to become one, you have to be born with the magic in you. It would have to come to you through me and Grandpa."

Papa began shouting. "Damn it, Meredith! If you keep on filling the kids' heads with that garbage, you're gonna turn them into a tribe of lunatics!" He slammed his fist on the table so hard that the cups and saucers jumped and rattled.

Everybody was momentarily stunned to silence, even Mama, because Papa seldom showed such a violent outburst of temper.

The children couldn't understand what all the fuss was about. They couldn't help being thrilled and excited, even a little pleased, that they had had a man like Grandpa Barnes, so famous and powerful, and even possibly evil, in their very own family. It made them feel special, in a way. It gave them something to share and be proud of. And in their secret dreams, they entertained obscure but enticing visions of worldly delights, fame, and riches that might lie in store for them someday, if they could truly inherit the powers of the Cunning Man and have a congregation of their own.

When Cynthia was nine years old, Papa went away on business and did not come back. For a long time, Mama would talk about his letters, making light-hearted small talk about what was supposedly in them, even though no letters actually came.

Mama began spending more and more time in the back room of her shop, poring over rare and expensive grimoires, books of magic, covering subjects such as divination, conjuration, and necromancy; the art of communicating with the dead. Something bad had happened to Papa and the family knew it.

There was very little money coming in. People no longer wanted to come to Mama's shop after finding out that they had to wait impatiently at the counter or browse through the place unserved while Mama stayed in the back room, totally absorbed in her books. She began to hoard herbs, potions, occult works, and ritualistic paraphernalia that might have been sold at a good profit. Papa had insurance but it could not be collected until he was proven deceased or legally declared so at the end of seven years.

Sometimes when the children came home from school or when they got up in the morning, the house would be full of the heavy, yet sweet smell of incense mixed with candle smoke. Mama paid less attention to their meals, their grooming, and her own housekeeping. They had few friends at school or in the neighborhood. Other kids started picking on Cyrus with increased frequency, intensity, and nastiness. His sister or one of his brothers had to walk him to the bus stop each morning to see that he got off safely to his special school and he had to be met again at the bus stop in the afternoon.

Desperate to help their mother in some way, Cynthia, Luke, and Abraham began working in the store after school and on weekends. This was partly because they didn't know what else to do with themselves. They felt like outcasts, rejected by the community. Many people referred to them as "the witch's kids" and either secretly feared them or openly made fun of them.

Working in the store, Cynthia began to read books on sorcery, spell-casting, and magic. She learned that a Cunning Man, like Grandpa Barnes had been, was, in reality, a white witch, with the ability to combat the power of Satan. But in the end, Grandpa Barnes had been overcome by a witch practicing black magic, as opposed to his own kind. According to Mama, in his old age, he succumbed to a stroke, the product of an evil spell cast on him by a rival witch who had gotten a lock of his hair. He knew it was no use to struggle, for the rival witch had stronger magic, and he predicted the time of his own death down to the very hour and minute. Did this not mean, Cynthia pondered, that black magic must be stronger than the other kind?

She hated her father for leaving Mama but she loved him too and wished he would return. Many a night she cried herself to sleep, hoping to see him bending over her in the morning, laden with the usual armloads of presents. Not having been raised in the ways of the church, Cynthia found herself "praying" to Grandpa Barnes to bring Papa back to her. The Cunning Man appeared to her once in a dream but when she tried to talk to him he vanished and she awakened. Repeatedly dwelling upon the meaning of this, turning it over and over in her young mind, she was struck by a realization of what Grandpa must be trying to tell her; that he was not strong enough to help her and her own spiritual resources were not sufficiently developed to stay in communication with him.

Every time she had the opportunity, Cynthia studied her mother's library of modern and ancient witch's lore, much of it seeming weird and incomprehensible to her at first. But it began to flesh itself out with meaning, to become more meaningful and real to her than her daily chores. Because she herself was distracted, Mama did not notice her daughter's intense absorption in matters that did not concern the average nine-year-old. In the shop Meredith would hobble past Cynthia, eyes straight ahead, as if her mind was far off somewhere, her arms laden with tomes she was taking to the back room to study alone, while Cynthia engaged in her own studies behind the counter.

Neither mother nor daughter paid much attention to customers anymore, or seemingly to each other, as their lives went on amid an array of herbs, potions, amulets, Tarot cards, altar cloths, grimoires, and other such equipment. Luke or Abraham waited on the few people who came into the place and played gin rummy, pinochle, or double solitaire between customers. Cyrus was easy to handle. He could remain busy for hours, doing the same things with the same objects, over and over. His favorite playthings were such items as voodoo charms and witches' bottles from the merchandise in the store.

Late one evening at about midnight, Cynthia was awakened by the odor of incense and flickering shadows cast by candlelight spilling into her room. Propping herself up on her elbows, she heard Mama's voice coming from somewhere in the house but could not make out the words. She tiptoed down the hall and saw what Mama was doing. Then she went to the boys' room and awakened them, her forefinger touched to her lips.

The children gathered around Mama at the dining table. She looked up at them but said not a word. To them, she seemed uncannily serene, preoccupied, yet intense and commanding. Her demeanor filled them with an unfamiliar solemnity and awe. She was wearing a black robe cinched at her waist with a gold cord and around her forehead was a wide black ribbon with a name inscribed upon it in shimmering golden letters: TETRAGRAMMATON. From her reading, Cynthia knew this was the usually unspoken name of the Spirit of the Universe.

The dining table was a large round one, and over it, centered, Mama had draped a black cloth with a magic circle printed on it in gold, inscribed with mystical symbols and formulae. Inside the magic circle next to an ornamental copper incense burner there was an iron retort, or witch's bottle, supported on a ring-stand over a lit candle, so that the substance being heated bubbled and seethed, transmitting its vapors throughout the semi-darkened dining room. The stench of urine, or something like it, was recognizable despite the efforts to overwhelm it with incense.

Cynthia realized that the words Mama was reciting came from *Lemegeton*, a medieval grimoire, the text of which lay open before Meredith at the dining table, which was now an altar.

"I conjure thee, Sheldon, my husband, the father of my children, that thou forthright appear and show thyself unto me before this circle without delay. I conjure thee by Him to all creatures are obedient, whether alive or dead, and by this ineffable name, Tetragrammaton Jehovah, which being heard, the elements are overturned, the air is shaken, the sea runs black, the fire is quenched, and the earth trembles. I invoke and command thee, O Spirit, to come from whichever place in the world thou art and give answer to my questions, answers that shall be true and reasonable. Come then, invisible form, and speak that I may understand thy words. Come visibly, before this circle, obedient in every way to my desires. By these holy rites, I conjure and exorcise thee, distressed Spirit, to present thyself here and reveal unto me the cause of thy calamity, where thou art now in being, and where thou wilt hereafter be. If thou dost not come or disobey in any ways, I will curse thee, and will cause thee to be stripped of all blessings and powers, and consigned to the bottomless pit where thou wilt remain until the day of judgment. I will cause thee to be bound to the waters of everlasting flame, fire, and brimstone. Come then, Sheldon, spirit of my husband, and appear before this circle to obey me utterly!"

The children kept their heads bowed, afraid of what might happen and yet desirous of seeing it. They wanted their magic to succeed in bringing a spirit into their midst. From time to time the smoke and the candlelight played tricks on their eyes so that something seemed about to happen. They thought they saw forms moving in the shadows. Cynthia was sure for a moment that her mother's magic was working. But eventually, for the boys, the excitement of anticipation wore off, their eyes began to go shut, their heads to nod. Cynthia, however, remained wide awake long after her brothers had crept away to bed, their mother not venturing to stop them.

"Why didn't it work?" Cynthia inquired at last.

Mama replied somberly, in a soft, persuasive timbre. "It may not work the way we would like it to. Magic does not always succeed completely because there are sometimes strong forces to overcome. But if we have succeeded partially, if Papa's spirit is trying to reach us, we may get a sign. He might be trying to break through sinister, evil forces that are surrounding this family."

"Well, why would they pick on us?" Cynthia asked, frightened.

"I don't know," Mama replied. "Perhaps it has something to do with Grandpa Barnes. Perhaps the witch who killed him put a curse on him and his descendants."

Three days later, on a Sunday, Aunt Edna and Uncle Sal were killed in a fiery automobile accident. They were on their way to visit Meredith and the children, having made arrangements for the occasion two days before by telephone. During the course of the call, they had tactfully expressed their worries about the state of Meredith's emotional health and her ability to cope with things. But an enormous tractor-trailer truck lost its brakes behind them on a steep, winding grade and pounded down on them, unable to stop, crushing their small foreign car like an accordion against a sheer rock wall. The driver of the rig and Edna and Sal were incinerated in the violent explosion which followed the impact.

It was not lost on Cynthia and her family, attending the closed-casket funeral, that Edna and Sal had been virtually cremated; the exact punishment ordered by Meredith to be brought down on the spirit of her husband if he failed to appear. Was this retribution?

One week after the burial, Meredith was summoned by her relatives' attorney to a disclosure of their last will and testament. All their property, money, and worldly goods were now hers, which amounted to the mansion eighty miles away, its contents and surrounding fifty-five acres, the chapel on the grounds, Sal's unsold paintings, contracts, and royalties, a savings account containing fourteen thousand dollars, and insurance policies totaling seventy-five thousand dollars.

In succeeding weeks, the decision was made to leave the town and the shop, for which they were paying rent, and go to live in Uncle Sal's and Aunt Edna's house. Her inheritances and the financial security that came along with them enabled Meredith to give herself completely to the occult. She could live off the insurance and the savings until the expiration of the seven years when her husband would be declared legally dead. Then she would get more insurance money and Social Security.

The family name had been Brewster, assumed when Meredith married Sheldon. But with the move to the mansion, Meredith began telling the children their last name was now Barnes, her maiden name while she was growing up in England, the daughter of Luke Barnes, the Cunning Man. "It's a name to be proud of," Meredith said. "In reclaiming it for ourselves, we lay claim to Grandpa's heritage, his powers."

Mama had discovered a trunk full of the Cunning Man's books and magical equipment in the attic. The stuff must have been shipped over from England when he died and Edna had never let on that she had gotten hold of it. Maybe she had been ashamed of it. She and Sal had often accused Meredith of being superstitious. In any case, it was quite an exciting find, and it occupied Meredith and Cynthia for days on end as they read through everything and then discussed their discoveries. There were many diaries and notebooks kept in the Cunning Man's own hand. Both mother and daughter, by this time, were deeply intrigued by witchcraft, its origins, and possibilities. Luke and Abraham were in awe of it and were believers in its potential power but they were content to allow Mama and Cynthia to become the experts.

Cyrus, who was fifteen at the time of the move, seemed to blossom in the country. It was as if the rural atmosphere; the outdoors and the absence of strangers in large numbers to nag and tease him, formed a more hospitable environment for his uncomplicated mental processes and abilities. He began to look more healthy and strong, if not more intelligent. He liked to pick flowers or catch butterflies. He never harmed the butterflies, always letting them go. One morning he found a dead bird and cried over it till Cynthia, trying to appease him, came up with the idea of having a funeral for it. She found a few scraps of wood and showed Cyrus how to make a small coffin. They went into the chapel, which had been Uncle Sal's studio, and made up a few prayers, which they recited. Then outside, in the small cemetery that had been the family plot of the overseer who had owned the place back before the Civil War, Cyrus and Cynthia dug a hole, tied two sticks together to make an upside-down cross, and had a burial ceremony that mimicked the Satanic one Cynthia had read about. After that, Cyrus was always looking for dead birds or mice that the cat had killed. He took to making small coffins in advance or saving shoeboxes to have in a pinch. Cynthia always helped him by reciting prayers and incantations over the tiny graves he dug.

None of the children was supervised. Meredith spent long hours upstairs in her room reading or feeling sorry for herself over the loss of her husband. She never ate much anymore and didn't cook either. The family subsisted on sandwiches, canned goods, and sometimes fresh fruit bought at the country store up the road or picked from fruit trees in the surrounding woods. Meredith began to look gaunt, sickly, even jaundiced, but the children grew accustomed to her deteriorated appearance. Without discussing it in so many words, Meredith and Cynthia both knew that they intended to try out some of the things that they had learned from Grandpa Barnes' notebooks. Nothing had been attempted since the day Mama had invoked Papa's spirit with disastrous results.

One day, to amuse themselves, Luke and Abraham rummaged around and brought out the traps Uncle Sal had given them for Easter two years ago. They jauntily made a foray into the woods to set the traps and could hardly sleep all night waiting for dawn so they could get up and go see. Cynthia and Cyrus went along too. One by one the six traps were checked but they were all empty. Luke angrily kicked a clod of dirt while Abraham hung his head and looked dejected.

"What kind of bait did you use?" Cynthia asked.

"Bread. We wet it and made dough balls," said Abraham.

"Huh! Who taught you to do that?"

"Nobody. I mean, I know you can use a dough ball to catch fish."

They all laughed, even Cyrus.

"I guess there ain't too many fish swimmin' through these here woods," Luke admitted.

"Why don't you use a carrot?" Cynthia suggested. "Then you might catch a rabbit."

"Yeah, at least we know what rabbits eat," Abraham agreed.

"One rabbit caught, and each of us could take a lucky rabbit's foot!" Luke exclaimed in gleeful anticipation.

After the change in bait, for three more mornings, all the children went out and checked the traps, only to find them empty. This was all the more frustrating because most of the time when they were on their way to the traps they would see plenty of rabbits and other game scampering around in the fields. Luke threw rocks at the animals but he never hit one.

"Shit! Wonder what these rabbits around here eat?" Abraham grumped.

"Lettuce, maybe," offered Cynthia.

"Gonna try it one more time with carrots," Luke pronounced determinedly.

"Why don't you let me work a spell for you?" Cynthia blurted.

They all stared at her. She knelt by the last trap they had checked, and with a stick, she drew a magic circle around it. Then she got some dew on her fingers and sprinkled in on the fresh bait. Bowing her head, still kneeling, she said the following words, paraphrasing something she had read in one of Grandpa Barnes' notebooks: "May the dewy tears of Almighty Tetragrammion, Lord of Creation, anoint the tools of the hunter. May the Spirit of the hunt bring food to our table. Amen."

"We're not gonna eat the rabbit, are we?" Abraham said.

Cynthia got up, brushing dirt from her jeans. "That doesn't matter, silly. The important thing is the charm. Tomorrow we'll see if it really works."

They went around repeating the ceremony over each trap and for the boys it got a little boring. But Cynthia was intensely excited, more so than she let on, for this could be a test of her power. Mama had told her that she could be the Chosen One of the family, because at birth a caul, a portion of her amniotic membrane, whatever that was, had remained covering her forehead, and according to tradition among white witches, this was a sure sign of tremendous psychic power to be vested in one so blessed. Mama had dried this membrane and kept it locked in her cedar chest, and she said that it must remain with the family forever and never be allowed to fall into strange hands, for the loss of it would bring dreadful results.

The next day they caught a rabbit. When they spotted it struggling in the trap, they all ran up and stopped short, out of breath, staring at it. They had run up whooping joyously but up close it wasn't a very pretty sight. The animal was weak from loss of blood; the mauled grass around it was streaked red. The rabbit's leg was bitten or gnawed down to the white bone, and still it remained locked in the steel jaws of the trap, vainly trying to pull free.

"Poor thing," Cynthia said, but an inner part of her was thrilled because the rabbit had been caught as a result of her magic.

For long moments the boys were speechless, in shock.

"Fun'ral," Cyrus mumbled. Tears were rolling down his chubby cheeks.

"What're we gonna do with it?" Abraham asked.

Nobody knew. It was one thing to dream about catching a rabbit but it was quite another thing to watch it die. Luke picked up a stick and hit the animal, trying to end its suffering but the blow did not suffice. The rabbit crawled in circles for a while then resumed pulling against the steel chain.

"Maybe we should let it go," Cynthia blurted before Luke could strike another blow.

"No, it's gonna die. Might as well put it out of its misery."

He swung the stick; thump! down on the quivering ball of fur, then thumped it again and again till it stopped quivering. Then he squatted so he wouldn't get blood on his trousers and unlocked the jaws of the trap. They all stood over the dead rabbit, looking at it in awe of its death.

"Gimme your pocketknife," Luke said to Abraham.

"What're you gonna do?" Abraham asked apprehensively as he handed the knife over.

"Skin it."

"You're kidding!"

"Nope."

Luke unclasped the long blade of the knife and stood over the dead rabbit, looking down on it. "I ain't no chicken," he said, as much to bolster his own courage as to convince the others.

"Wait!" Cynthia called out. "He's my rabbit as much as yours. I want some of his blood."

"What for?"

"For magic."

Luke and Abraham waited while their sister went home to get a witch's bottle and Cyrus went along with her to fetch a shoebox. Filled with lurid fascination mingled with queasiness and fear, the others watched while Luke sliced the rabbit's jugular vein and drained some blood into Cynthia's bottle. She wiped off the bottle with Kleenex, corked it, and put it safely in her pocket. Then, with nobody like Uncle Sal around to act as teacher, Luke made a horrible mess of his attempt to skin the rabbit, and in the end, they put the bloody, mangled pieces; pelt, bones, and carcass into the shoebox.

In the little cemetery by the chapel, Cyrus used his toy shovel to dig a grave. After the burial and the placing of an upside-down cross on the mound of earth, Cynthia knelt and recited: "Almighty Tetragrammaton, we beg you to accept this sacrifice which we now offer to you so that we may receive your blessings. We ask you to bless our deeds that we perform in your Almighty Name. Consecrate the blood that you have given us this day, that it may further your holy work, for we ask only to serve you, for ever and ever. Amen."

Mama heard about the incident in all its gory detail that evening after supper. She seemed in good spirits and listened keenly, though the children kept interrupting each other to get it all told. It was one of those rare occasions when Meredith had troubled herself to cook a full meal, including a cake for dessert made from a boxed mix.

She said, "The power is in you then, Cynthia, as I had suspected. Grandpa Barnes has chosen you as his receptor, the bearer of his blood lineage. If you prayed over the trap and consecrated it, then whoever you found in it the next morning was your enemy."

"A rabbit?" Abraham blurted.

Mama shot him a cold, withering look. "Evil spirits, demons, can assume any shape," she instructed in stern, serious tones. "It is not uncommon for them to take the guise of a rabbit. Though they may appear quite harmless outwardly, this is only a devil's trick, and you must protect yourself by destroying them. It's the only way to counteract the evil power inside them."

In the following weeks, the Barnes children redoubled their efforts in setting traps and torturing, maiming, and killing the animals that were sent to them. These were mostly squirrels, raccoons, possums, and rabbits, with an occasional stray dog or cat. It became a challenge to see who could devise the most ingenious, painful ways of dealing with these enemies. The children grew callous about performing amputations and decapitations, searing live flesh with fire, gouging or poking out eyes, and mutilating genitals. No amount of cruelty was too extreme for the evil spirits embodied by these apparently harmless creatures. Luke and Abraham did most of the killing, while Cynthia presided over the ritual aspects of their activities and Cyrus did the burying.

And one day the inevitable happened; a human being was caught. At least it looked like a human being. The children heard the creature's screams as they walked along the dusty road about a hundred yards from their house. They stopped in their tracks, listened, and knew that the screaming was coming from out in the field where they had set several of the largest traps. This was truly frightening, potentially the largest thing they had yet caught. Afraid of what they might find, they took their time about heading into the field. Cynthia began praying to Tetragrammaton to protect them. All of a sudden Luke took off running, out toward the middle of the field, having first grabbed Cyrus' shovel out of his hand. Whatever it was they had caught, it was behind some tall weeds. Luke went crashing through the weeds, Cyrus huffing and puffing behind.

Luke was standing over the body of a boy. There was a lot of blood. The steel jaws of the trap had nearly severed the boy's leg and Luke had apparently split his skull open with Cyrus' shovel.

"Is he... is he dead?" Abraham managed to gasp out.

Luke was still breathing hard. "Don't know." He took a rapid series of deep breaths. "No. I guess not. Look! He's still breathing."

Luke raised the shovel over his head to hit the boy one more time.

"Wait! That's Jimmy Peterson!" Cynthia said.

They all came around to look at the boy's face, trying to see his features through the smeary mask of fresh blood. Jimmy Peterson was the son of the man who operated the country store several miles up the road. The Barnes family didn't have any love for the Petersons. Both father and son, and even Jimmy's little sister liked to poke fun at Cyrus whenever they saw him, calling him "dum-dum" or "weirdo." Luke had fought with Jimmy once and Jimmy had won by giving Luke a bloody nose.

"It's him, all right," Abraham said.

Cyrus nodded his head, his eyes wide.

"Wonder how long he's been caught," Abraham mused.

"But it ain't really him, is it?" Luke said.

"Don't make no difference anymore," Abraham intoned in a near-whisper. "He done stopped breathin'."

They all looked and saw that the boy was dead.

"We all know that it's not really him," Cynthia said with assuredness. "And now that he's not alive anymore, he doesn't even look like Jimmy."

"True," Abraham agreed.

"He must have been sent to us like the others."

So they dug a grave and buried him, like any of the animals they had caught before except instead of using the cemetery on their property, they dug a hole in the woods and Cynthia recited incantations over his grave. His remains were buried deep and out of sight forever, except for a bottle of blood which Cynthia needed, and one of his front teeth, a dead man's tooth, which, according to a passage in a medieval grimoire she had read, was absolutely indispensable to the working of certain powerful spells. In fact, in one of his diaries, Grandpa Barnes had written that no magic at all could be entirely dependable without the vital ingredient of a dead man's tooth. When the children got back to the house for lunch, they told Mama what they had done. Luke started it by saying, "We caught something big today and we took care of it like you said."

A few weeks later, the second demon in the guise of a human was caught in a trap out in the same field. This one looked like Jimmy Peterson's sister. For a while, it almost tricked them into not killing it but Mama was behind them this time and she wasn't fooled. She broke the demon's spell.

"Hit it!" she yelled. "I told you, they can take any form they want to! Hit it, Luke! Don't let it get the upper hand on you!"

The demon screamed and screamed till Luke's shovel blade smacked into its face and skull. It fell down, and Abraham and Luke both kept beating it for a long time. When it was dead, it didn't look like Jimmy Peterson's little sister anymore. Copying Luke and Abraham, Cyrus took up the shovel and hit it, too.

"You did real good," said Mama. "Now Cyrus can make a coffin and we'll have a funeral."

When the thing was buried, Cynthia said the prayer over its grave: "Almighty Tetragrammaton, we ask thee to help us in the destruction of our enemies, as thou has done today. We pledge ourselves to thee and will continue to be thy faithful servants. Whomsoever thou send to us, we shall destroy, knowing it is thy will. Amen."

CHAPTER 6

Nancy was afraid of the boys who had picked her up in their van. They both seemed a little wild or maybe they were just trying to impress her. They said they were fraternity brothers from some college in Massachusetts and they were going to Fort Lauderdale for Easter. Thousands of kids would be swarming on the beaches, "having a ball" according to Tom Riley and Hank Bennet. Tom, the driver, was sort of good looking, with light brown hair parted in the middle, long, sharply etched sideburns, and a touch of acne around his mouth and chin. His buddy, Hank, was a tall, lanky black, with a wary look in his eye and a protruding Adam's apple.

Nancy didn't say much, hoping they'd understand that she was not as free and easy as some girls. It was impossible to carry on any extended conversation anyway with the tape deck in the van blasting Rolling Stones music. Nancy liked her music loud but the volume in the vehicle was so excessive she could envision the cilia in her ears bending like waves of grass in a strong wind. She had read you could permanently impair your hearing that way.

For better than an hour she had stood hitchhiking at an intersection near the outskirts of town. Cars kept passing her by and each time she was terrified one might contain her mother or her stepfather. She kept her thumb out, looking awkward and feeling that way, for she had never hitchhiked before. Her suitcase was at her feet by the curb, along with her guitar in a leather case.

"Out of sight! You play guitar!" Tom had exclaimed when Nancy first climbed aboard.

She played clarinet in the band at school, but she didn't take any pride in it; instead, she prided herself on her folk singing. A few weeks ago she had entered the annual talent contest for seniors, singing a ballad about true love versus sexual love, self-consciously taking the edge off the understanding and sense of pathos in her voice, afraid of letting students and faculty know that she had personal experience with the song's subject matter. Still, she had won second prize. It meant more to her than her good grades or anything else she had achieved in high school. There was a message in the folk ballad she hoped had penetrated to her ex-boyfriend.

Where was she going to go and what would she do with herself? Standing on the corner with her thumb out, she wanted to break down crying. By running away from home, she'd miss out on graduation. Could she get a diploma later? She didn't know. She had an older sister, Terri, who had gone off on her own to California a few years back to try to become an actress, and now she was working with a repertory theater group in San Francisco. Nancy supposed she could try to get to the Coast, too, to dump her troubles in her sister's lap and hope Terri wouldn't send her back home. She didn't want to face her stepfather ever again but she was a minor, under eighteen. Couldn't the authorities make her go back to her mother if they caught up with her before her eighteenth birthday? If so, she would have to tell what had happened, and if her version was believed, she'd be responsible for wrecking her mother's marriage.

With these thoughts tormenting her, she was startled to see that a late-model green Cadillac had pulled over to the curb, and a man leaning across from the driver's side was pressing a button, making the window wind down. He was a fat, balding, middle-aged man in a plaid business suit who reminded her of her stepfather. "How far you goin', honey?" he called out, his voice low and hoarse as if he had smoked too many cigarettes.

"C-California," Nancy replied uncertainly.

"That's quite a long trip. What sort of arrangements might we make if I agree to take you as far as six hundred miles of it?"

"What do you mean?"

"Don't play coy with me, young stuff. I'll make it simple for you. Three hundred miles today; then we share a motel room. Tomorrow another three hundred miles, another motel room and we kiss each other goodbye in the morning with no hard feelings. That way your conscience is clear; you've paid your way. I'm only going as far as Detroit but you'll be a good chunk closer to where you want to go. You headed for LA. or Frisco?"

"F-Frisco. "

"Better put some flowers in your hair," the man joked, chuckling coarsely. "Mister, you better get out of here or I'll call a cop." Nancy threatened. Then she added, ironically; "My stepfather is on the police force!"

The man sneered. "You smart young slut. If I had hair down to my ass and beads around my neck, you'd jump in here in heat and tear your clothes off." He hit the gas pedal hard and peeled out, leaving Nancy alone by the curb, backing away, shaken.

Down the block in their van, Tom and Hank were stopped at a red light. Looking in the rear-view mirror, Tom said, "Hey, Hank, the young chick is still back there on the corner. The guy in the Cadillac didn't pick her up. I'm going back for her."

"For Chrissakes! Forget it, Tom! There'll be plenty of chicks in Lauderdale. She'll probably tear open her blouse and threaten to yell rape to the nearest cop if we don't hand her all the money we got in our wallets."

"You worry too much. She's probably just a nice young chick who needs a lift. I—"

"C'mon, white boy," chided Hank sarcastically. "Don't be so naive. Most of the time if a fine-looking piece like that has to go begging for something, it means she's in some kind of trouble. Either that or she is trouble. Why you want to mess up a good vacation?"

The light changed to green and Tom executed an abrupt right turn instead of going straight ahead. Hank looked dismayed but Tom ignored him, saying, "If we don't pick her up, she's liable to get picked up by some creep."

"All right, you're the driver. But I sure hope you ain't doin' somethin' dumb." As the van rounded the block, Nancy was standing once more with her thumb out, more timidly than before. Tom smiled brightly when he saw her there. Instead of stopping by the curb, he pulled into the lot behind her so she'd be on his side of the vehicle and he could talk to her without being obstructed by Hank.

"Hi!" Tom called out above the blare of music. "Need a lift?"

Warily, Nancy asked, "Didn't you go around the block once before?"

Tom grinned. "Yeah. I wanted to pick you up the first time but you appeared to have your problem solved."

"Oh, sure, all my problems would've been solved for good. All I had to do was let that man take me to a motel. Is that what you're after, too?"

Angrily, Hank scoffed, "I told you, Tom, the chick's nothing but trouble."

But Tom persisted, talking to Nancy with sincerity. "Look, me and Hank, we're not creeps. We give you a ride, you don't owe us anything. I'd hate to see you get picked up by a lunatic, that's all. We're heading down to Lauderdale."

"I wanted to go to my sister's place in California," said Nancy, wavering. "Okay, let her go," Hank blurted.

"Wait a minute!" Tom argued. Keeping his eyes on Nancy, he said, "Why don't you come down to Florida with us? Have a really good time for a few days. Lots of college kids down there. After Easter, you should easily be able to catch a ride west with someone your own age."

"What makes you think so?"

"Kids'll be going back to college to finish out the term. A good many of them make the jaunt to Lauderdale from schools in the Midwest and so on. You'll be able to check out a potential ride for a few days on a personal level; make sure it's somebody safe."

"Well..." Nancy hesitated, biting her lip, telling herself that if these two boys were decent, being with them was probably better than being totally on her own.

"Come on," Tom said, persuading her.

She made up her mind and got into the van.

Bert Johnson sat at the kitchen table over a cup of black coffee while his wife prattled on and on about her experience at the hairdresser's. What she was saying made little impression on him. He was too worried about where Nancy might be and what she might do next. He should never have gone after her, whether she was leading him on or not. He had let the booze get hold of him. Now he could lose his marriage, his job, and his reputation if Nancy opened her mouth about what had happened. Bert was wearing a small bandage on top of his forehead over the spot where his stepdaughter had clouted him with her portable radio and he hoped the excuse he had ready would suffice when his wife asked about it.

Looking at herself in a mirror in the hallway, Harriet said, "So he cut my hair shoulder length, styled it a little differently, and frosted it less than last time. It's not as light as Nancy's, though. Where'd you say she went? I had the impression she wanted to take your car to the mall."

"As far as I know, she did go to the mall," Bert said. "She wasn't here when I got home. One of her girlfriends must have picked her up early."

Harriet went to the breakfast counter and poured herself a cup of coffee. "Probably she went with Patty. She's not dating anyone new, is she?"

Bert shrugged. "How in the world should I know? I can't pretend to keep track of that wild crowd she hangs around with sometimes."

Mrs. Johnson brought her cup of coffee to the table and sat down across from her husband. Putting in double cream and two sugars, she said, "I don't think Nancy and her crowd are particularly wild. In fact, they're pretty nice compared to many teen-agers nowadays."

"Don't worry, they know what it's all about," Bert said, grimacing. "Some of them could teach you and me a wrinkle or two."

"Bert, whatever do you mean?" Harriet purred, the implied meanings in her husband's tone having aroused her sense of curiosity and scandal.

"Don't ask me to tell you, Harriet."

As he intended, this caused her to crease her brow and pout worriedly.

"Nancy isn't everything you think she is," he said, as if confessing it reluctantly.

"I think you had better explain yourself," she challenged.

"Well, I've been debating for a long time whether I ought to say anything. But I suppose it's best that you know. She pretends to be very sweet and innocent when you're around but it's only an act. She's been flaunting her little body at me, rubbing up against me whenever she gets an excuse, and I've been trying to avoid her because I have no idea what her game is. I think she wants to break you and me up."

While he was talking, Harriet's expression had gone to disbelief and shock, and for a long moment, she stared at her husband, stunned, not able to find words to express herself. Her voice came out finally in a near-whisper. "Bert, are you saying what I think you're saying; that Nancy had tried to seduce you?"

Skillfully, he backed off from his accusations, rendering them more believable. "I don't think she wants it to go that far. Maybe she's just testing her sex appeal... or something... in a juvenile way. I have no doubt that she's still a virgin."

Harriet drew in a deep breath. Then: "I happen to know that she's not. She was heartbroken when her boyfriend dumped her and I happened to overhear one of her phone conversations that made it pretty clear she had given herself to him."

Bert shook his head sadly.

"She won't confide in me," Harriet said. "I have to learn everything by accident. Not that I expected her to remain a virgin, she's too pretty. And this isn't the nineteenth century. Sex is out in the open and our children grow up too fast, way too fast. What was I supposed to do with Nancy, keep her locked in her room?"

"I'm afraid it's too late for that already," Bert lamented. "It could be that she resents the fact I'm not her real father. Maybe she wants to destroy me and get back at you too, Harriet, at the same time."

"Bert, you must be imaginin' things. I'm not going to believe this nonsense for one minute. After all, Nancy is my daughter, my flesh and blood."

"All right, Harriet, if it makes you feel better to bury your head in the sand. Why do you suppose I've had to start hittin' the bottle again? It's because of your daughter. Till now I couldn't bring myself to break it to you. It's such a terrible thing to have to face. So I've been trying to shield you from it and doing my best to stay away from her. I was even glad that she wasn't here when I got home."

Harriet did not reply, her mind in turmoil. Could it be that Nancy was actually the way Bert described? Harriet had been hurt deeply by her first husband because she had closed her eyes to his infidelities in the face of evidence, intuitive and otherwise. That should have convinced her something was wrong. She was always too trusting, too ready to accept people at face value, especially those close to her. She expected from them the same honesty that she gave. After her divorce, she had learned not to be disappointed by the worst in people when it finally came to light. But her own daughter? The idea of Nancy doing the things Bert said was repugnant, unreal, no matter how hard Harriet tried to allow for the possibility that it might be true. Because of being a working mother for so many years, Harriet didn't feel that she understood her daughter as well as she should.

If push came to shove, who should she believe, Nancy or Bert? She didn't want to lose Bert. Before he came into the picture, loneliness and penny-pinching had taken their toll on Harriet's confidence and self-respect. Bert represented companionship and security for her old age. Offspring couldn't be depended upon. Look at Terri, off on her own in California already, and maybe a letter from her once every six months, unless she found herself needing money, and then she suddenly knew how to write. This was the first installment on the reward for working hard to raise two daughters all those years without a husband and father in the house.

Well, Harriet thought, she'd have to talk to Nancy about this and get her side of the story. Perhaps it was all an innocent misunderstanding of some sort. Looking up at her husband, Harriet noticed his bandage and inquired solicitously, "Bert, did you get hurt on duty last night?"

Glad that she had thought of it herself, Bert used her lead to follow through on the excuse he had planned all along. "I had a run-in with a punk who was drunk and disorderly. Not too serious of an incident, really. Al and I got the cuffs on him and hauled him in."

"Did Al get hurt, too?"

"Are you kidding? Does Al ever have bad luck? Not a scratch on him, as usual."

She reached out and put her hand on his. "Bert, you and I haven't had much of a scx life lately. Could it be because of what you've been going through with Nancy?"

From the moment this explanation had occurred to her, she had clutched at it, willing to believe in it rather than blame herself for a failure in the bedroom.

Bert pressed her fingers in his and gazed at her balefully. "What do you think? I love you, honey, and I don't want to lose you. One of these days Nancy might come to you with some wild stories, trying to put the blame on me. I just want you to be aware of my side of it first so nothing can ever come between us. Naturally, we have to give Nancy love and understanding but the important thing is for you and me to stick together."

Overcome by Bert's sincerity, Harriet's eyes smarted and a tear rolled down her cheek. Even if Bert was partially to blame for this crisis, she didn't want to lose either him or her daughter.

By this time Nancy, Tom, and Hank had crossed the Pennsylvania border into West Virginia. Hank was smoking a cigarette. Nancy was sitting rather morosely in the back seat of the van, still overcome by her troubles, although Tom had been trying to cheer her up. Reaching to the dash to turn down the volume, he commented happily, "Dig all these mountains without a trace of green on them yet, except for a scattering of pine; I love it! Tonight we'll be camping in the Blue Ridge Mountains, maybe on the Shenandoah River. Do you know the song 'Shenandoah,' Nancy? Maybe you can sing it for us. Then the next day or the day after we'll all see the scenery turn greener and greener the farther south we go, all the way to good old Florida."

"Goin' where the weather suits my clothes," Hank drawled.

"I'm staying in my bathing suit the whole time!" Tom said exuberantly.

"Say somethin'," said Hank, turning to peer inquisitively at Nancy. "We give you a ride and you put a damper on things."

"I'm just tired," she apologized.

"Man, how tired you gonna be by the time we go another thousand miles?" Hank challenged.

"I'm hungry," said Tom, changing the subject.

The speed limit slowed to thirty-five; they had come into a rural hamlet in southern West Virginia. Hank turned the rock music up loud as the three youths sized up the town they were cruising through. The place was called Cherry Hill, one more in a succession of colorfully named West Virginia towns like Man, Cabin Creek, Hundred, and Nitro. Cherry Hill had a large general store, a feed store, several rough-looking saloons, and a place that sold mining equipment. People walking on the narrow main street all seemed to be dressed as farmers, miners, or hunters. Parked outside the saloons and stores were several pickup trucks with racks full of rifles and shotguns mounted in their rear windows.

"Wow! What a haven for rednecks!" Tom said. "We better watch ourselves out here, Hank."

"Why?"

"Some of these hicks would just as soon blow us away as look at you."

"You been seein' way too many movies. My parents came up from Tennessee. They said the South ain't nowhere near as mean as it's portrayed."

"Still, I don't think we should try anything," Tom said, and Nancy's ears perked up as she wondered what he had in mind.

Hank told Tom, "Sometimes you're a chicken-shit, you know that? Nothing out of line ever happens in a one-horse town like this. If you're smart and you got balls, you can get away with damn near anything."

Made extremely apprehensive by this kind of talk, Nancy asked, "What would you want to get away with, Hank?"

Glancing at her sideways, he said, "Anything. I mean—" He caught himself and fell silent for a moment, then said to Tom, "You gotta realize some of these hick places don't even keep their deputies on duty after midnight."

"What is this all about?" Nancy demanded.

Haltingly, Tom explained, afraid of the impression his explanation might make on Nancy. "I might as well tell you, as long as you're going to be riding with us. Me and Hank, well, we're not exactly what you could call rich. Hank has a football scholarship but it doesn't pay his full tuition and I have to struggle by on what my parents give me plus what I earn waiting on tables in the fraternity dining room. So we sat down and figured out a careful budget before we left campus. If we paid for our gas, we wouldn't have enough money to buy food, and if we bought food, then we wouldn't have money to pay for gas. So we made up our minds we'd just have to steal groceries all the way from Massachusetts to Florida. That's how we've been makin' it. If you don't want to stick with us now that you know, we'll let you out and you can hitch another ride."

"After you talked me into going to Florida instead of California!" Nancy complained in exasperation.

"How much bread you got on you?" Hank inquired sharply.

"Uh, fourteen dollars."

"Certainly not enough to feed yourself all the way to Frisco." "No, but..."

"Then you have to steal," Tom concluded. "And if you have to, then it isn't a sin."

To Tom, Hank said, "Did you spot any lawmen so far?"

"Uh-uh."

Nancy slumped in her seat, wrestling with the moral implications of what had been discussed. She was just beginning to like Tom and Hank and feel safe with them and now this. She had little doubt, though, that it was only one of a series of scary adjustments she'd have to make now that she had left home.

"Here's a nice grocery store made to order," Hank said, showing how much he relished the discovery by emitting a low, throaty chuckle. He was pointing at a chain food-store on the right-hand side of the road and Tom pulled over and parked the van with the engine running.

"You could help us pull this off," Hank said to Nancy.

"You don't have to if you don't want to," Tom stated emphatically, turning to face her after flashing a glance at Hank.

"But if you stick with us without doin' your share, you're gonna be eatin' stolen food, anyway," Hank pointed out.

A few minutes later, Hank and Nancy entered the grocery store, sauntering past the checkout counters. She wheeled the shopping cart down an aisle to begin shopping. "Let's make this a real spree," Hank said with a mischievous grin, then started tossing items into the cart. Joining in the lark after a moment of panicky hesitation, Nancy soon got caught up in the swing of things, and it was strangely liberating. She and Hank piled their cart high with anything and everything they could grab off the shelves; meat, cereal, cocoa, eggs, butter, bread, cheese, condiments, potato chips, pretzels; whatever struck their fancy. They found themselves laughing uproariously and tossing things back and forth to each other as they sped down the aisles weaving around regular customers who stood and gawked.

The cart filled, Hank and Nancy wheeled over to the checkout counter. The woman behind the checkout counter, a prim-looking old biddy, checked, tallied, and bagged their selections, ringing them up and holding out her hand for money. "Just a minute, I want to return this cart," Nancy said.

Meanwhile, Hank had picked up two armloads of groceries and was already moving toward the exit. Wheeling her way through the checkout aisle, Nancy pushed the empty cart into an area where it would temporarily obstruct pursuit by the woman behind the counter, then snatched up the remaining bag of groceries and ran behind Hank out through the automatic door and toward the van, which Tom had kept waiting outside, doors open and engine still running. The woman screamed and hollered for the store manager as Nancy and Hank made their escape.

They piled into the van on the run, strewing stolen groceries all over the back of the vehicle. The van lurched out and began speeding away but immediately a siren started wailing, a police car was in pursuit.

"Gas it!" Hank yelled.

Nancy cowered in the back seat, trying belatedly to get her seat belt fastened. Hitting sixty miles per hour, the van left the outskirts of Cherry Hill, attempting to outrace the police siren.

They were on a rare straight section of two-lane blacktop, heading into sharp curves. Nancy screamed and Hank yelled, "Look out!" because Tom was going too fast to make it. But he didn't attempt the curves. Instead, he careened off, humping and bumping into a farmer's field. A dirt road ran through the field and Tom got on it and there were fewer bone-jarring bumps. The police car still followed, some distance behind. When Tom caught sight of it in the rear-view mirror, it spurred him to go faster. The dirt road had a hard-packed surface but there were plenty of bends and twists. Still, Tom barely slowed down. Whoever was driving the police car was more cautious, for the police were not in such close pursuit as they had been before.

The road wound through a valley of poor, rundown farms, few and far between. In a blur, Nancy watched unpainted barns and farmhouses flashing by every once in a while among the trees. Foliage, collapsed fences, and branches sometimes whipped against her window because the road was so narrow and Tom kept swerving from one side to the other in his effort to go fast and still control the vehicle. Every once in a while there would be a narrow turn-off but they'd shoot past it too quickly to do anything about it.

Finally, Tom took a chance and slowed down. When a turn-off came up, he took it, hoping to lose the cops. As soon as he was around the bend, he gunned it, hoping they wouldn't be able to spot his dust. In a little while, the sound of the siren seemed farther away. Tom kept driving as fast as possible for a few more minutes. Finally, he slowed to normal speed, looked over at Hank, and burst out laughing. Hank and Nancy laughed too. The laugh felt cleaner and fresher than anything Nancy had experienced in her life. Was this the joy of thievery? The hard-driving chase had been terribly frightening. But now that they had gotten away clean, a sense of exhilaration set in. They laughed their heads off, not wanting to stop. As they began to recover, Tom turned to Hank, momentarily taking his eyes off the road.

"Wow! What a rush! I'd love to have been with you two in the store. I—" "Tom! Look out!"

As Nancy screamed, Tom swerved the van to narrowly avoid hitting a man at the edge of the dirt road. The man, large and brawny in farmers' bibbed coveralls, had stepped out into the van's path, and he was carrying some sort of long, bulky bundle wrapped in a soiled blanket. As the van swerved, the man ducked back into the cover of woods from whence he came. He continued to stare stolidly after the van, still supporting the bundle in his arms.

In the van, Tom said, "Damn! I almost hit that guy! Whew!" Perspiring, he wiped the back of his hand across his forehead.

"He was carrying something," Hank said. "Did you see that?"

Tom chuckled nervously. "I was lucky I saw him at all. Thanks for yelling, Nancy."

She ran her tongue over dry lips then spoke in hushed, anxious tones. "There

was something creepy about him. I got a look at his face and he seemed to be grinning, even when it looked like you were surely going to run him over. I swear, he had some kind of strange smile on his face. And I think I saw a shoe sticking out from under his blanket." She shuddered from her imaginings.

Hank turned around and laughed at her. "Naw! He was just a big farmer with a bundle. You're shook up, girl. Your mind's playing tricks on you. Soon as we find a good place to camp, we'll smoke some grass to loosen you up."

Nancy stared out the side window, mulling this over. She had tried marijuana once with no results; she had failed to get high. She wasn't particularly against trying it again. But in the company of two strange boys? How loose might they expect her to get?

The man with the bundle watched the van going away, stirring up dust, disappearing around a thickly wooded bend in the distance. Then he stepped ploddingly back into the middle of the road. He was a broad, beefy man with a leering smile on his face. A corner of the soiled blanket fell away from his large bundle, revealing the lower part of a bare leg, and one foot wearing a red high-heeled shoe. The man continued to stare down the road, in the direction of where the van disappeared. Blood ran down the calf of the dangling leg and dripped off the tip of the red shoe.

CHAPTER 7

They parked the van in a field by a stream and camped for the night. They went through the bags full of stolen groceries, delighted with the pile of goodies now that they had a chance to really look it over. "We won't have to steal anything for another few days," Hank said. Nancy was glad to hear it and she helped Tom separate out the perishables like milk, eggs, and cheese, and pack them into a Coleman ice chest in the back of the van. In the last waning half-hour of dusk, the two boys gathered dry twigs and fallen timber and built a small campfire. Then all three had a supper of ham-and-cheese sandwiches and hot cocoa.

Afterward, Hank rolled several joints, lit one, and passed it to Nancy without a word as he held in his drag. She didn't feel like arguing so she took it and inhaled deeply. Noticing her slight hesitation, Tom said, "You ever smoke grass before?" Still holding in the smoke, she nodded her head yes as she handed Tom the joint. She didn't tell him that she had not succeeded in getting high and didn't expect to this time. Tom dragged on the joint then passed it to Hank and it kept going around till it was finished. Then Hank lit another one and passed it. "This is real good dope," Tom said sagely.

Nancy giggled wildly and realized with a shock that she was stoned. Tom and Hank looked at her knowingly and laughed too. "It's so nice to relax around the fire at home after a hard day of shopping and being chased by creditors," Hank said, and his comments seemed hilarious. The threesome laughed and laughed. Tom exploded a lungful of smoke that his laughing forced out of him as he once more handed the second joint to Nancy. It was so short it burned her fingers. "Gimme the roach," Hank said. And taking an alligator clip from his pocket, he used it as a roach holder so they could continue smoking the thing down to nothing.

When it was too small to hold between his lips, Hank held the glowing remnant next to his nostrils and sniffed the hot vapors. Then he lit the third joint and handed it to Nancy. Really stoned now and enjoying the euphoria of total abandon, she continued to take drags every time the joint came her way. "I got the hungries," Hank said, his eyes crinkling in the orange glow of the campfire as he rubbed his stomach and giggled. All three were ravenously hungry because of the marijuana, and they went into the back of the van and brought out crackers, jelly, peanut butter, apples, bananas, potato chips, and pretzels, and root beer to wash it all down.

For a long time, they ate, trying the peanut butter and jelly on crackers, potato chips, pretzels, apple slices, and chunks of banana. Because they were stoned, it was all wildly delicious. Every once in a while Tom or Hank tossed a log on the fire. "Beats the hell out of bein' back on campus," Hank said. "When we get back, it'll be time to start crammin' for finals." "Oh, what a bummer," moaned Tom. "Did you have to remind me, Hank? Huh?" "What's your major?"

Nancy asked. "Psychology," Tom told her. "Let's change the subject. Sing something for us, why don't you?"

Feeling uninhibited, Nancy got out her guitar and sang a black spiritual, "All My Trials." Tom thought she sang wonderfully and enjoyed watching the seriousness and the emotion in her young face. He was beginning to be attracted to her romantically. Hank noticed this and for some reason, it irked him. He and Tom had set out for Lauderdale to have a ball, not get hung up on one chick.

If Tom lost his head over this girl, as he was giving every evidence of doing, it was clear to Hank that their trip would be much less of an enjoyable adventure. Hank would be on his own, unpaired, looking for strangers on the beach to get to know and get involved with. And they would mostly be white strangers. Although he told himself to stay cool, Hank couldn't help but feel that in some unplanned, accidental, and unforeseen way, his buddy, Tom, was in danger of copping out on him.

Strumming on her guitar, Nancy finished the last chorus of the spiritual: "If religion was a thing that money could buy, the rich would live and the poor would die. All my trials, Lord, soon be over, all my trials, Lord, soon be over, all my trials, Lord, soon be over." Letting her voice trail off with the concluding cords, she leaned her guitar against a tree and sat back self-consciously, wondering what they had thought of her singing. She was pretty sure Tom liked it but she had no idea about Hank.

"Nancy, you sing nice," Tom complimented. She

smiled and thanked him, feeling pleased with herself. "I don't think you got much right to be singin' a slave song," Hank jeered angrily. "Come on, Hank!" Tom snapped back. "Don't start getting paranoid on us." Hank eyed Tom coldly, lighting up a regular cigarette instead of another joint. "Who's paranoid? Not me. I just said I don't think a white girl ought to be singin' a slave song, that's all."

He made a great show of being calm and aloof by laying his head back and slowly blowing a chorus of smoke rings. "Black people paid their dues in that area, not whites. A white chick like Nancy can't have the least idea of the feelins' behind the black spirituals that deal with slavery." Tom shook his head in disagreement. "That's pure bullshit, Hank. What's gotten into you? Every time something's eating you that you don't want to be upfront with, you cover it with silly-ass rhetoric. Next, you'll be telling me an Italian can't sing an Irish ballad."

"You don't like me, do you?" Nancy said to Hank. Hank looked over at her. With an air of having made a very shrewd deduction, he told her, "It dawned on me that you got to be runnin' away from home. And if so, me and poor, innocent Tom are accessories. How old are you?" "Nineteen." But she immediately gave up on the lie. "No, I'm seventeen, almost eighteen." "Sure you ain't sixteen or fifteen?" "Leave her alone, dammit, Hank!" Tom shouted. "Shut up, white boy. One of us has to have the sense to find out how much hot water we may be in. You ever hear of the Mann Act?" "Come off it!" "Transportin' a minor across state lines. You better think about it, Tom. We could have the F.B.I. on our asses." "Bullshit, Hank! I know you want to get into law school but you're not there yet. Now come off it."

To Nancy, Tom said, "Hank gets mean sometimes when he's stoned, but it doesn't last, so don't worry about it." But Nancy wanted to speak for herself. "If you're uptight about me, Hank, you don't need to keep me around. I wouldn't want to be a burden to you. We can go our separate ways in the mornin'." But she didn't get through without crying; a tear rolled down her cheek, glistening in the firelight. Tom came to Nancy and put his arm around her. "Hank doesn't mean it, Nancy, honest. Dammit, Hank, tell her you don't mean it. Now you've gone and made her feel bad." "I do mean it. We hardly know this chick. I warned you she'd be trouble."

Crying, Nancy got to her feet and headed off into the woods by herself, picking her way along the path by moonlight. Tom jumped to his feet too. "You're the one who's trouble, Hank. I wish you'd learn to keep your big mouth shut. Tomorrow when you're not stoned, you won't even remember what a hassle you caused."

Chasing after Nancy, Tom found her sitting by herself at the edge of the stream. He stopped behind her, a few feet away, looking down at her. She did not turn around to face him. "Mind if I sit with you?" he asked. She flipped a pebble out into the water, watching it splash and ripple. Since she still hadn't said anything, Tom took a few steps toward her and laid a comforting hand on her shoulder. "Wouldn't it help if you told someone your problem?" "What makes you think I've got one?" she blurted defiantly. "If you haven't got one, there's no need to talk about it," he admitted. Then he sat down beside her.

She kept staring straight ahead. Tom told her, "I just want you to know, Hank really isn't a bad guy. He'll let you stay with us, you'll see. Everything will be okay in the morning." "I don't want to be a burden," Nancy said quietly but determinedly. "I just want to get to my sister's house in California and I'd rather not come between you and your friend. You'll get along better without me." "That's not true at all," Tom insisted. "You've been helpful and... and fun to be with. I want you to stay with us, Nancy."

She didn't know what to say. Despite efforts to the contrary, she had started crying again. Tom opened his mouth to tell her not to cry, and at that moment both he and Nancy heard a noise from back in the woods which caused them both to whirl around. Tom shouted, "Hank! Is that you?" There were more sounds of someone tramping through the brush and suddenly the footsteps stopped. Tom and Nancy listened, getting a bit frightened. Tom called out once again, "Hank? Hank, is that you?" No one answered.

On their feet now, Tom and Nancy peered all around but the moonlight could not penetrate some of the denser patches of woods. They strained their eyes to see into the foliage from where the footstep sounds had seemingly come. Just when it appeared that the surrounding woods had fallen completely and permanently silent, a low, throaty chortle came from somewhere and Nancy jumped and grabbed onto Tom. "Probably some kind of animal," he said, trying to be reassuring. "A hyena, maybe, if they have them around here, or else Hank's playing tricks.

Come on, Nancy, let's get back to the campfire and turn in. We'll want to be on the road early tomorrow and I hope you'll decide to still travel with us. I like having you around. I mean it." Feeling scared and needing the comfort of his nearness, Nancy allowed him to escort her back along the path in the moonlight, away from the stream. Peering from behind some branches, the man in bibbed coveralls watched them go, grinning. He liked the girl real well. She was very pretty and he couldn't wait to look at her up close, and touch her, and feel her long, blonde hair.

Bert and Harriet Johnson were up late worrying about Nancy for different reasons. It was almost time for Bert to go out on the midnight shift so he was in his uniform. Harriet was in pajamas and a bathrobe. She had waited until after the eleven o'clock news, then had placed a few phone calls to Nancy's friends with unsatisfactory results. No one could shed any light on her whereabouts. When Bert picked up his lunch bucket and came over to kiss Harriet goodbye, she said, "Something happened between you and my daughter, didn't it? You've been lying to me, Bert, and I want to know why? Why didn't Nancy come home?"

Believing firmly that righteous anger was his best defense, Bert exploded, "How the hell should I know? I told you the kid isn't as innocent as you make her out to be. She could be out carrying on someplace." "It's not like her to stay out this late without phoning. I'm worried about her and I think you know something you're not telling." Bert looked hurt and insulted. "For

Chrissakes! You've got a fantastic imagination! I've got to get down to the station. I'll check the blotter when I get there if it'll make you feel any better. If anything's happened to Nancy that the police know about, I'll get the information. By the time I call you, she'll probably be safe in bed." "I certainly hope so," said Harriet, relenting.

Bert kissed her goodbye and went out, slamming the door. Harriet went to the liquor cabinet, poured herself a good stiff drink of bourbon, and gulped half of it down. She carried the remainder with her into the bedroom, where she sat on the edge of the bed, feeling wrung out. It looked as if she might have to choose between her daughter and her husband, and she didn't feel capable. She had never been a strong person and this sort of emotional strain was too much for her. She downed the rest of the bourbon, set the glass on the nightstand, and noticed a bottle of sleeping pills there. Snatching up the bottle immediately, she shook out some capsules and swallowed them, then lay on her back on top of the covers, a nightlight burning in the bedroom.

She was jarred out of the drug-induced sleep by the ringing of the phone. She groped for it and answered groggily. "Hello? Nancy?" The voice on the other end of the line said, "This is your husband, Bert." "Oh, Bert," Harriet said coming to her senses, "have you any news?" He said, "I just heard from Nancy. She says she's at one of her girlfriend's houses. She's staying over." "Which girlfriend?" "I don't know. She must've said but I don't remember. I guess I didn't catch it. You do feel relieved though, don't you honey?" "Yes, of course. But why didn't she call me at home?" "She said she tried to call. Claimed she must've dialed the wrong number but I think that was just an excuse to make us think she tried to get in touch earlier. She was probably in the middle of something, you know how teenagers are, and never even thought about phoning till late."

"Oh, I suppose so, Bert. Thanks for letting me know. I'm sorry I was angry with you." "No problem. Goodbye now, honey. See you in the morning." Bert hung up the payphone, satisfied that his lies had worked to confuse the issue, at the very least. If Nancy had run away from home, which is what he suspected, for he had found her suitcase and some of her belongings missing, then tomorrow when she still didn't show up, he'd say that, obviously, her phone call of this evening had been a trick designed to throw him and her mother off the track. In the meantime, Harriet would calm down and stop badgering him.

If Nancy was merely staying with a girlfriend and had phoned him about it as he had indicated, then how could something bad have happened between them? Bert's only problem would be if Nancy chickened out and came back home but by then, he'd strengthened his position and sown so much confusion that Harriet wouldn't know who to believe. Bert hoped Nancy would stay away for good. That way his position would be safest. When he thought about what he had done, he felt ashamed, threatened, and frightened. If Nancy ever brought charges, even if he were acquitted, the scandal and gossip would be enough to wreck him.

Not long after sunrise, Nancy awakened at the campsite. She had spent the night curled up in a sleeping bag Tom had loaned her. The morning was cold and damp, the nylon bag wet with dew. Tom and Hank were still asleep in their sleeping bags, not far from the now-dead campfire. Nancy eased herself out of her bag and moved quietly away from the campsite, alone. She walked along the path for quite a ways till she got to the edge of the stream where she and Tom were last night. She hunkered by the stream, contemplating her reflection in the water.

Her hair was matted and damp. She wished she had brought a comb, brush, and towel along so she could wash her face and fix her hair. She still hadn't made up her mind whether to stay with Tom and Hank or chance it on her own. In a pensive, indecisive mood, she picked up a few pebbles and dropped them into the stream, letting them fall out of her hand slowly, one by one.

Back at the campsite, Tom and Hank were still sound asleep in their sleeping bags. They did not hear the footsteps sneaking up on them through the woods. Finally, both Tom and Hank were prodded in the ribs by heavy, brown boots and they jumped up, startled to see gun barrels staring them in the face. They had been jarred out of slumber by two sheriff's deputies brandishing service revolvers.

"Hold it, fellows!" one of the deputies barked. "Don't make any foolish moves. Keep your hands visible." The second one said, "If either of you tries to reach into his sleeping bag for a gun, I won't wait to find out what you're reaching for. I'll just shoot." In a shaky voice, Tom said, "What's this all about, officer?" In the back of his mind, he figured it must have something to do with the stolen groceries. "Shut up!" the man covering Tom snapped, pointing his pistol at Tom's face. The other deputy suddenly gave Hank a savage kick in the ribs. The boy screamed and writhed in agony, imprisoned in his sleeping bag, while both deputies chuckled.

"A bug in a rug," one of them sneered, and they both went on laughing. Tom stared up at them, wide-eyed and frightened. The deputy standing over him was tall and powerfully built, his tight lips and piercing black eyes set hard and mean. The second deputy was shorter and more wiry with a perpetual scowl on his face. Both wore tan uniforms with heavy, brown boots and wide-brimmed hats. The tall one had sergeant stripes on his sleeves. The other was a corporal.

"Where's the girl?" the corporal demanded harshly. "You killed her, didn't you?" "Filthy, sadistic scum," the sergeant added. The short wiry corporal lashed out with his boot, dealing Tom a kick to his ribs. Tom yelled in pain and terror as Hank continued to moan softly, staring up at the deputies in scared bewilderment. The sergeant planted his boot squarely on Tom's chest and aimed his gun between Tom's eyes. Tom whimpered, still hurting badly from the kick in the ribs. "Shut up, goddamn you!" the deputy warned. "Stop making a spectacle of yourself or I swear I'll blow your brains to bloody pieces!"

The corporal chuckled softly, "Maybe they think they can pin us with a police brutality rap. Niggers especially take the cake in that department, don't they?" Emphasizing his point, he prodded Hank with his boot in the sore spot where he had kicked him. "These filthy scum don't deserve humane treatment," said the sergeant. His foot still on Tom's chest, he applied pressure demanding, "What'd you do with the girl, you maniac? Where'd you hide her body?"

He stepped up onto Tom, putting all his weight on the boot that was pressing into the boy's chest. Tom gritted his teeth to stop from crying out but let loose a slight whimper despite his efforts, making the sergeant angry. "Don't you scream. I told you, I'll blow your fucking brains out!" He jammed his revolver up against Tom's forehead, threatening to pull the trigger. Grinning meaningfully the corporal said, "Maybe we ought to drag them back into the woods one at a time, and question them separately." "Good idea. Which one should be first? Eeny, meeny, miny..." He waved the barrel of his weapon back and forth from Tom to Hank. "Catch a... nigger by the..."

"Wait!" Hank cried. "Can we talk about this? We didn't kill anybody. There was a girl with us but she must've cut out in the middle of the night." Through his pain, Tom said, "All we're guilty of stealing a few bags of groceries." The corporal chortled exuberantly, "Oh-ho, a confession! Trying to get off lightly by admitting to a lighter offense, no doubt. Well, it won't work. We've heard that ploy before, right sergeant?"

The sergeant pursed his lips thoughtfully. He said, "I'm tired of playing games with you two. We know you're guilty. Your van was spotted near the place where that poor girl was found raped and stabbed to death. You can't lie your way out of it. We have to make you pay and we don't much care if we bring you in alive or dead." "We're entitled to a trial," Hank insisted. "We're innocent!" He knew why they were picking on him, he thought, but it didn't make any sense for them to be so down on Tom. The short, wiry one gestured with his revolver, "Get your asses up out of those sleeping bags, pronto! Which one are we going to question first, sergeant?"

Tom pleaded, talking desperately, "No! I just remembered. We saw a big, heavy man in farmers' bibbed coveralls. I almost ran him down; he was standing right in the road. He was carrying a heavy bundle. It could have been a body! It must have been one. Is he the one who turned us in? If so, you can see he was trying to divert suspicion from himself. My father's a lawyer back in Boston. He..." But neither deputy apparently believed Tom's story, for they both started chuckling. The chuckling turned into derisive laughter as Tom and Hank crawled out of their sleeping bags and stood in front of the dead campfire looking hurt and helpless.

Nancy, who had come back from the stream, was hiding behind some bushes about fifty yards away, observing what was going on. At first, she had been alarmed by noises of scuffling and arguing coming from the direction of the campsite. Then when she saw the two policemen, she was afraid they were out to arrest her and bring her home so she stayed in concealment, hoping to learn more about the situation.

To her amazement, she saw Tom and Hank being

handcuffed. The corporal seized Hank's handcuffed wrist and yanked him in an about-face. Hank trembled, feeling totally at these unreasonable men's mercy and reaching a point of panic. All at once, he started to run, trying with all his energy to get away. The corporal crouched, sighted, and fired twice. Hank crumpled and hit the turf, sliding on his chest and face, then lying very still.

Tom yelled, "You killed him, you stupid redneck! You didn't need to do that! We're innocent! Innocent, goddamn you!" His face was a mask of rage and anguished helplessness, and bitter tears rolled down Tom's cheeks. He made a move to go to Hank but the sergeant made him stay in one place by jabbing him severely with his revolver. Standing over Hanks' body, the corporal gave a long glance back at Tom, a faint, wry smile on his face. Then he took careful aim at Hank's head and squeezed the trigger. The loud report all but blotted out Tom's scream. Then there was silence.

After a moment, the corporal said, "I warned the spade he'd get his head blown off but he had to try me. Serves him right, the young punk." Dazed and rapidly going to pieces, Tom mumbled, "You must be crazy. Crazy." "Come off it!" the sergeant barked in his loudest tone yet. "Your buddy was resisting arrest. You want to try the same? I guarantee you you'll end up the same way too. You ready to confess to raping and killing that girl? I knew her and her family, see. I'm willing to go to any lengths to bring in her killers. People in this county will turn their heads to any irregularities as long as they feel they got justice."

Practically screaming, Tom said, "But I tell you, I'm innocent! What proof could you possibly have? This is all so cockeyed. I don't understand it. Let me call a lawyer, please. One innocent life has already been lost." Still watching from her hiding place, Nancy was terribly frightened. Rooted there by fear, she was not about to show herself. She wanted to do something to help Tom but she was powerless, at a total loss, and she hadn't heard enough of what was said to really understand the situation.

The corporal came over to Tom and jammed his gun into the boy's abdomen. "You ready to confess or do we have to beat it out of you?" Tom's dilemma was beyond his comprehension. He spoke weakly in a near whisper, "You might as well kill me too. That's what you're going to do, aren't you?" The Sergeant replied sternly, "Well, we know you're guilty so actual confession is merely a formality. The fact that your partner tried to run doesn't make you look very innocent? Me and the corporal like to save the taxpayers' money every place we can." "Yep," agreed the corporal.

Again he prodded Tom with his gun. He jammed the weapon hard, over and over into the boy's ribs, making him cry out painfully. "Why don't you run too?" he suggested diabolically. "How much of this kind of treatment could you take before you decide to run?" The sergeant pointed his revolver at Tom, saying to the corporal, "Step aside, gimme a clear shot." Tom trembled and closed his eyes. Without further ado, the sergeant pulled the trigger, shooting Tom in the chest. As the boy sagged and fell, the sergeant fired again, then again. Tom lay on the ground not far from Hank, both bodies bloody messes.

From her hiding place, Nancy screamed and started running in total hysterical panic. Both deputies wheeled and spotted her simultaneously. The corporal instantly crouched and aimed, ready to fire, but the sergeant stopped him, shouting, "No! Take the girl alive. We want her alive. Don't get carried away now. After her!"

The two deputies started running, trying to catch up with Nancy. She plunged into the woods on the far side of the clearing, running and running for all she was worth. The two deputies kept coming after her at a steady trot as if they were not particularly worried that there was any real chance of her getting away. They kept plodding after her relentlessly, waiting for her to tire herself out. Every time she looked back they appeared to be just over her shoulder. She couldn't seem to lose them, though she tried to put her last ounce of energy into it out of fear and desperation.

Nancy broke out of the patch of woods onto a dirt road, a section of the one the van had traversed yesterday. She ran down the road, looking behind her now and then to see how close her pursuers were, screaming for help now and then, and looking frantically for someplace to hide. When the two deputies got out onto the road, Nancy seemed to have gained on them, but she had merely disappeared around a bend.

For a moment, this confused them as to which way she may have gone and they halted, peering and up and down. They soon realized she couldn't have gone right or she'd be visible on the straightaway. They took off running to their left, toward the bend in the dirt road. They put on speed, loping along, making up lost distance. Both men were now breathing hard but their pace was still relentless.

Nancy spotted a red brick house with white columns set far back off the road. She ran across the vast lawn and up onto the veranda and beat fiercely on the front door, and tried to open it, but it was locked. She yelled and yelled for someone to come and let her in. No one answered. She ran around the side of the house and up on the steps of the back porch. In a panic, she yanked at the door which was stuck, but it finally gave way and swung open. Nancy dashed into the house, slamming the door behind her and locking it with the sliding brass bolt.

She found herself in the kitchen. She looked all around, breathing hard, amazed at its vastness, taking in at a glance, the enormous colonial fireplace. Then her eyes fell on a huge mahogany highboy filling one corner of the kitchen. Taking quick strides toward the piece of furniture, she pulled open a drawer and in her haste overturned it. Silverware clattered out onto the floor, making a tremendous racket, hurting Nancy as it struck her on the legs and feet. She dropped the drawer with a loud, resounding crash.

Nancy stooped and rummaged feverishly among the silverware on the floor but to her dismay, there were no knives, only forks, and spoons. This was as odd as it was disappointing. She needed something with which to defend herself. Pivoting sharply, she headed for the front of the house, crossing the threshold of a large, elegant dining room, only to be brought up short upon seeing a young woman in a white dress, sitting at the dining table, engaged in a game of solitaire.

This strange young lady, about Nancy's age, with comely features and black hair worn in a tight bun, laid a playing card face up on the table and gazed at Nancy placidly. Nancy stammered, "I, uh, thought nobody was home. I was calling for help. Why didn't you hear me? Do you have a telephone?" The young woman did not reply to any of this as Nancy's momentum carried her into the room. "Are you deaf?" Nancy wondered out loud. Still getting no reply, she darted her eyes beyond the woman at the card game and saw into the next room and immediately let out an ear-shattering scream.

In frozen horror, she stared into the living room where two mangled corpses were hanging from the cross-beamed ceiling. The bodies were those of men, clothed only in bloody underwear. Each corpse had four or five knives protruding from the various parts of the anatomy, which explained the absence of knives in the kitchen. Because she was so horror-struck by the sight of the dangling bodies, at first, Nancy didn't see that the demented man in bibbed coveralls was in the living room also, standing just behind and to the right of the corpses. He had in his hand a large butcher knife which he was sharpening on a whetstone. He smiled at Nancy as she continued screaming, terror rooting her in her tracks.

The young woman at the dining table played another card, calmly laying it face up, red on black, as if nothing of unusual interest was going on around her. Nancy bolted and ran; the man with the butcher knife taking a step or two after her. She unbolted the kitchen door and ran out into the backyard, straight into the arms of the two deputies who instantly pounced upon her, wrestling her into the ground and pinning her arms behind her back.

While the deputies were busy subduing Nancy, a hand reached out and pulled the kitchen door shut, and the man with the butcher knife did not come out of the house. Hauled to her feet by the two deputies, Nancy struggled and babbled hysterically, "Oh, please, let me go. I... You killed my friends, both innocent! The real murderers are in there!" She stared at the closed door of the house, her eyes flashed wildly. "Well, now," said the sergeant, "let's have a look. Got to investigate; see if this young lady's telling the truth."

He and the other deputy began dragging Nancy up onto the back porch. She screamed and dug her heels into the ground, trying with all her might to resist their pulling her along. "No! Please!" she cried. "I don't want to go in there!" The corporal said to the sergeant, "She's stark-raving mad, I'm afraid. Doesn't want to come along with us and prove her innocence. Maybe she's lying."

The two deputies pushed open the back door and dragged Nancy into the house. She fought back, grabbing onto the doorframe, but they methodically punched her hands loose. Finally, they knocked her down and pulled her across the floor by her ankles, through the dining room where the young woman playing cards looked up disinterestedly, and into the living room where the two corpses hung from the rafters. The man in bibbed coveralls chortled, watching the girl he had spied on yesterday being dragged helplessly over the living room carpet.

At the far end of the large room were three wire cages, of the sort used to cage and transport show dogs. In one of the cages was a young woman, wild and disheveled-looking in her underwear, who cowered in her cage as Nancy was being dragged across the floor. The other two cages were empty. The man in bibbed coveralls, still chortling, moved to one of the empty cages and opened the door for the two deputies who were maneuvering Nancy into position. As she lay flat on her back in front of the open cage, one of the men, the corporal, straddled her and laughed and started pulling off her jacket and blouse. When she resisted, he slapped her face.

The man in bibbed coveralls looked on leering and chortling, swishing his sharp butcher knife through the air above Nancy's head. The other girl cowered and cried in her cage while Nancy was being beaten and undressed down to her bra and panties; the three men flinging her garments around the living room. The undressing completed, Nancy was forced into a cage and the wire door was locked. The man in the bibbed coveralls pranced insanely around the cage, laughing and grinning, prodding Nancy from one side to the other by jabbing at her with his long-bladed knife. She alternately screamed and cowered, trying to avoid being stabbed.

For a time, the two deputies enjoyed this game, elbowing each other in the ribs with amusement. But at last, the sergeant spoke up, "Enough! Enough Cyrus! Look at the mess you made in here!" He pointed disapprovingly at the hanged bodies. "We have to get this house cleaned up. Mama doesn't like it like this. You know she's got a bug for keeping things tidy." The two deputies pushed the man in bibbed coveralls ahead of them out of the room, and fear-ridden, Nancy watched them go.

For the first time, she noticed the holes in the backs of the deputies' shirts, streaked with dried blood, and she knew for sure now that the real deputies were hanging from the ceiling. She shuddered. Her situation was hopeless. She had fallen into the hands of a quartet of homicidal maniacs. In her agony, she broke down sobbing, throwing herself down onto a ragged, musty quilt on the bottom of her cage, and in a while, due to exhaustion and shock, she lost consciousness. Her last thoughts were of Hank and Tom. The girl in the other cage watched her sleep.

In the next room, Luke Barnes, still in his deputy's uniform, stood before his sister, Cynthia. She was nineteen now. It had been ten years since they had killed their first demon. Cynthia, eerily pretty and pale, her pallid complexion accentuated by her bun of coal-black hair, looked up from her game of solitaire. Luke said, "Sister, you've got to help us straighten up the house for Mama's sake, or else Mama is going to be mad."

Cynthia eyed her brother sternly. "You had better go up and talk to her, Luke. You know darn well she's going to chastise you for killing that other girl ahead of time. Mama told us we're supposed to have three for the Easter services." "I'll have another by Good Friday," Luke promised. "I'm not about to let the whole congregation down." "But now we've got to go out and catch us another one," Cynthia complained. "And catching them is the dangerous part, people are liable to get wise. You and Cyrus and Abraham know that. How many times did Mama tell you?" Chagrined, Luke said, "I'll go up and talk to Mama as soon as the living room is cleaned up. We're not in any trouble yet. Mama won't yell at me for no reason, you wait and see."

When Nancy came to, opening her eyes slowly and recoiling from the shock of her surroundings, she found the girl in the other cage looking at her piteously. "My name is Gwen Davis," the other girl whispered. "They killed my sister." Gwen stifled a sob. She was about twenty-five years old, probably attractive, if not so beaten up and scared. Her brown hair was plaited into two pigtails that made her look girlish so that you had to look closely to get an idea of her true age. One of the pigtails was tied with red ribbon but the other ribbon had been lost, no doubt in a struggle with her captors, and the ribbon-less pigtail was coming undone.

"The two deputies, the real ones," Gwen said, "maybe coulda saved us but they're hanging from the rafters. You and I have to pull together, figure a way to get out of here before they kill us." "How are we going to do that?" Nancy said hopelessly and she started to sob, burying herself in the ragged quilt on the bottom of her cage. Luke, Abraham, and Cyrus clomped into the room. Nancy kept her head and eyes buried and continued to cry softly while they went about the business of cutting down the bodies and getting them out of there.

Luke and Abraham were in jeans now. Luke backed his pickup truck out of the garage and kept it parked in the driveway with the engine idling. Abraham and Cyrus came out of the front door carrying the body of one of the slain deputies wrapped in a blanket and heaved it into the bed of the truck. In a little while, after going back into the house, they came out with the second body, also wrapped up, and laid it into the truck too. Abraham and Cyrus then squeezed into the cab of the pickup truck and Luke backed it out of the driveway.

Cynthia came out on the porch and watched the truck go, churning up dust, then went back into the house, shutting the front door behind her. She started cleaning up the living room, every now and then glancing at Nancy and Gwen. "Let us go," Gwen tried, but Cynthia only chuckled. "But you're a young girl like us," Gwen said. "Surely you must have some feelings for what we're going through. How can you condone torture and imprisonment?"

Cynthia came over to Gwen's cage. Gwen looked up at her, thinking how young and pretty she was, her figure so lithe and girlish. It just didn't seem possible that she could be as evil and perverted as her brothers except for the intense gleam of her black eyes, which lent her face a scary kind of radiance despite the paleness of her complexion. Looking down at Gwen, she said, "I'm not like you. Don't ever try to tell me that. I have special powers, a congregation of my own.

They believe in me. You'll see for yourself, come Friday at midnight when the services start."

"What if I believed in you too?" Gwen asked. "Could I be part of your congregation?" She was hoping to continue a dialogue that might cause Cynthia to waver and perhaps think about letting her and Nancy go. "It's too late for you to be saved," said, Cynthia. "A false profession of faith will not fool me."

The pickup truck pulled into the camping area where Tom Riley and Hank Bennett had been shot to death. The white van was still parked there, the sleeping bags strewn all around. Luke, Cyrus, and Abraham got out of their truck and laid the bodies of the two slain deputies on the ground on top of the cold embers of the campfire. "Good place for a burnin'," said Luke. "Nice and secluded. They couldn't have picked it better for us."

"Burn 'em and bury what's left," said Abraham. "Start digging a hole big enough to hide the leftovers, Cyrus."

Luke and Abraham dragged over the bodies of Tom and Hank, making a pile of corpses. They covered the pile with blankets, sleeping bags, and miscellaneous gear from the van. The deputies' uniforms were thrown on the pile too. At last, Luke poured a can of gasoline over it all, then struck a match and started a bonfire, a funeral pyre. The faces of the three brothers, Luke, Cyrus, and Abraham were highlighted weirdly by the roaring flames.

CHAPTER 8

Cynthia lay in bed reading from a book entitled *The Appeal of Witchcraft* by Dr. Morgan Drey, a professor of anthropology at New York City College:

It is no accident that the devil is portrayed in medieval woodcuts as a cloven-hooved beast with his tongue in the shape of a triple penis. Sadism is a sexual perversion and a belief in witchcraft is the horrid sickness of a sexually repressed society. The inquisitor and the witch are both perverted by the belief, by the insistence by church and state, that witches do indeed exist as agents of the devil and need to be rooted out, punished, and destroyed.

The individual becomes either witch or witch hunter because it gives him an outlet for his perversions. In saying 'I am a witch,' one gives license to oneself to indulge in lascivious, erotic practices running to the obscenity of sadism; in saying 'I will persecute witches,' one gives oneself license to treat the witches sadistically. In either case, human beings torture, maim, and kill each other in an orgy of righteousness and unrighteousness, holiness and unholiness, till the two sides of the coin become one: both witch and inquisitor, operating within the witchcraft mystique or matric, give vent to impulses which are sadistic.

This duality of holiness transmuted to unholiness was personified by Gilles de Rais, the soldier-protector and rumored lover of Joan of Arc. In 1429, when their mystical triumphs on the battlefields had resulted in the coronation of Charles VII, Joan was revered as a saint and Gilles was made a Marshal of France. He was only twenty-five years of age, had inherited enormous wealth, possessed a love of books, music, and poetry, and was extremely handsome and famous. In the language of today, Gilles 'had everything going for him.' He went home from the wars with the intention of leading a life of genteel beauty, luxury, and good works.

But in 1431, through treachery, Joan of Arc was condemned as a witch and burned at the stake. This event, coupled with several other key disappointments in Gilles' life, seems to have torn his brain loose from the moorings of sanity. He left his wife and renounced all future sexual intercourse with women. Withdrawing to his castle, he surrounded himself with an army of soldiers, sycophants, homosexuals, and perverts, He began to squander his wealth by traveling around the countryside with a sumptuously armed and outfitted entourage and by sponsoring lavish public entertainments which rivaled some of those staged by the fabled Roman emperors.

Gilles, in fact, felt an admiration and kinship with the most depraved and corrupt of the Romans; Nero and Caligula. He pored over prized books in his vast library which were filled with woodcuts elaborately depicting the emperors' excesses of lasciviousness, brutality, and torture.

As Gilles' coffers were being depleted by his profligate lifestyle, he hired a sorcerer and alchemist, Francesco Prelati, to aid him in transforming lead into gold. Many medieval alchemists used their "art" as a pretext for debauchery and perversion, and Prelati was no exception. He convinced Gilles, after a few futile experiments, that no real progress would be forthcoming without making a pact with the Devil.

Gilles lured a young boy to his castle, raped him, then tore out his eyes, mutilated his genitals, and ripped out his heart and lungs. Gilles used the boy to vent his sexual appetites and Prelati used the blood and organs in alchemical experiments. Thus began a period of eight years in which Gilles, goaded by Prelati, raped, tortured, mutilated, and dismembered literally hundreds of children. When he was finally arrested and sentenced to be hanged and burned, and the prosecutor asked him the reason for his hideous crimes, he replied, "Truly I had none but the gratification of my passions." This was an amazingly candid admission by Gilles, who would be expected to rationalize his behavior by telling himself that the young boys had to be killed, anyway, for the all-important purpose of turning lead into gold.

Most of the time aberrant behavior needs an excuse, a justification. Religious fanaticism gives birth to witchcraft by encouraging a deep-rooted fear of a very real Devil who walks the earth and possesses living persons. It was once said that nothing is so healthy for religion as a strong, unshakable belief in Satan.

What priest today wouldn't secretly love to meet Satan in person, to be confronted with incontrovertible proof that the Prince of Hell does exist and therefore the lifelong devotion to a priestly calling has not been a futile waste of energy?

Having come to the end of a chapter, Cynthia laid down the book and thought about the author, Dr. Morgan Drey, whom she had met at her store in Greenwich Village. He had come in to purchase books for research and artifacts he could photograph to illustrate *The Appeal of Witchcraft*. When the manuscript was published some months later, he had returned to present her with an autographed copy and ask her to let him take her to dinner. She surprised herself by saying yes.

She had not opened the store to get involved with non-believers. It had been her idea to go to New York and run a place of her own, specializing in the sale of witches' paraphernalia, potions, and herbs, much like Mama's old store so that she could meet other people with beliefs similar to her own. She did not care to meet skeptics like Morgan Drey. She wanted to use the store as a way of building her own congregation. Over a period of four years, she had been successful in developing a conclave of almost two hundred witches from various parts of the United States. Each year the services took place at midnight on Good Friday, Holy Saturday, and Easter Sunday. Special rites, pulled off at considerable risk, were looked forward to by all. Some of the members of the congregation were gaining followers of their own and conducting services regularly in other states and cities but the services in the chapel on the Barnes family estate were by far the grandest and most daring.

Morgan Drey had interviewed Cynthia for his book. She had been open with him, except where self-protection made discretion imperative and had even told him, rather proudly, about her own congregation and the annual services conducted under her leadership. Over a sip of wine in the Italian restaurant where he had taken her, he chuckled good-naturedly. "Surely you don't really believe in all this," he told her. "I can realize that you have to maintain avidly that you do for the benefit of your customers but you can tell me the truth. What are your private feelings?"

Her eyes met his across the table. He was a good-looking, if scholarly, man in his late twenties. His forehead was high and Cynthia knew this was a mark of intelligence. He had light brown hair, deep-set inquisitive blue eyes, and a scrupulously trimmed goatee and mustache.

"My private beliefs are as I have said," Cynthia told him. "I believe in my own powers."

"What powers?" he challenged. "What proof do you have that you've ever worked any extraordinary magic?"

She clenched her teeth, her eyes flashing with annoyance. "I cannot tell you," she said, haughtily angered.

"You mean there is nothing," he persisted.

"I mean I can't tell you," she uttered coldly. "These matters are not to be discussed lightly with a non-believer. "

"You know, you're very pretty when you get worked up," he said, changing the subject and continuing to stare at her intently.

She knew intuitively that he liked her and more. He wanted to get involved with her romantically. This was pleasing but also frightening. He reached out and took her hand, but she drew it away as if it had been burned, and her cheeks flushed red from embarrassment.

"W-What's the matter?" he said, startled.

"Nothing. I…"

"Are you afraid of men?"

"No."

"Do you have a boyfriend, a fiancé?"

"Certainly not."

"What do you mean, certainly not? As if the mere idea were out of the realm of possibility?"

She did not answer. He had her unsettled.

"You had better be careful, Cynthia," he warned. "Or else these beliefs of yours will become a horrid obsession. You're much too young and pretty not to have a normal life, one free of anxiety and repression. You need to fall in love someday and have children."

"Never," she said fervently. "I have other things to do which are more important."

"Let me see you again," he pleaded. "I'm attracted to you. I'd like a chance to change your mind, to show you another way of thinking. That mother of yours, I know you love her, but she has given you some warped ideas. And 1 believe you have a hostility toward men because you were deserted by your father ten years ago and you've never gotten over it."

His words shook small tremors of self-doubt in Cynthia, making her angry. How dare he! What gave him the nerve to be so impertinent? She would never allow him to undermine her confidence, her commitment. Her congregation was proof of her sanctity. They worshipped her because she had inherited tremendous spiritual gifts from her grandfather and great-grandfather. She had the power of the caul, the mark of Tetragrammaton, who had chosen her to be even greater than her ancestors, the Cunning Men.

"I would appreciate it if you would never come to my store again," she told Morgan Drey.

He immediately looked hurt, baffled, his usual aura of self-assuredness gone. She had succeeded in wounding him instead of the other way around. The triumph was hers. She smiled at him to make his pain worse. She had to get him out of her life so she could go on leading her congregation. He was a stupid and dangerous non-believer. She did not need him. There were others who cherished her for the proper reasons. When she needed a man or men, she could choose from among those who had the truest, deepest, most violent ability to please her.

What did Morgan Drey know? His book was nonsense, full of theoretical babbling. What would he think if he saw the rituals in person? He would go stark-raving mad; his pitiful imaginings dwarfed to ridiculous pettiness by the real thing.

An extraordinary idea occurred to Cynthia; what if she could convert him? The possibility was titillating. She knew he was attracted to her; maybe there were reasons he didn't want to admit. Perhaps he wasn't as skeptical as he seemed to be. His writings about Gilles de Rais, Jack the Ripper, and the Marquis de Sade might be an outlet for a side of himself he barely understood, a potential yearning to be set free. Skeptics made the most passionate converts once they were shown the way to the actual, rather than the vicarious, indulgence of their passions. Judging from his writing, Morgan Drey seemed particularly fascinated by Elisabeth Bathory, the sixteenth-century Hungarian countess who kept hundreds of young girls chained in the dungeons beneath her castle so she could periodically renew her own vigor and beauty by slitting the young girls' veins and bathing in their blood. What would Morgan think if he knew that some of the countess' practices would form the basis for rituals of Cynthia's devising which would commence in two days, on Good Friday, when the entire congregation had arrived?

She laid down his book and closed her eyes, shutting him out of her mind. She wondered about the girls downstairs who were going to be unwilling contributors to their rituals. What sort of lives did they lead? Did they have boyfriends? Lovers? Were their sexual preferences normal or bizarre?

From across the hall, she could hear the muffled tones of Luke's voice droning on, talking to Mama behind her closed bedroom door. "Mama, I hope you've gotten it out of your head that I'm to blame for doing wrong. We didn't mean for that girl to die but she went and hurt Cyrus pretty bad and you always said he had a delicate temper. It was the girl's fault.

Me and Abraham, we're gonna catch another girl tomorrow. We got us a van that don't belong to us, nobody can trace it to us. Tomorrow morning we'll take it out on the road and we'll find us another girl, I promise. Maybe it'll be somebody young and pretty, maybe a virgin. Don't you worry now. Me and Abraham, we ain't gonna disappoint the congregation."

Mama didn't say anything. She just sat in her rocking chair, looking out the window. Luke didn't know if she was angry at him or not. Hoping that he had his mother's approval and understanding, even though she didn't voice it, he backed sheepishly out of the bedroom and shut the door. Then he went down the hall to his own room and started getting undressed for bed.

Downstairs in their cages, Nancy and Gwen were talking, keeping their voices low. Gwen tried to remain calm while explaining how she had been trapped. "My sister and I were driving by, exploring the back roads, and..." she stifled a sob, "...and Sally, she liked to hunt for old cemeteries, the older the better, to take pictures and make tombstone rubbings. Right away she noticed the family graveyard out back, across the field, so she wanted to stop and look. But she wouldn't dare go out there without asking permission. We got out of the car and went up on the porch to knock, and the door banged open all of a sudden and the three brothers jumped us. It was awful. Awful! I didn't do a good job of fighting back, I was in shock or something. Sally bit and scratched and they had a hard time with her. She kicked Cyrus, the big crazy one, between the legs and he roared like a wounded bear, and then he stabbed her, again and again. I was half out of my mind, already in my cage. I…" Gwen buried her face in her hands and broke down crying.

Nancy trembled, not knowing how to comfort the older girl. She said, "I'm sorry, Gwen. Please, maybe you shouldn't talk about it anymore."

But Gwen went on as if she had to get it all out of her system. She was thinking it out as she talked, trying to get it all straight in her mind, reciting details that refused to yield to reason or understanding. "The two deputies stopped here. I could hear them talking out on the front porch. They said they had been chasing a white van that had gone speeding away from a grocery store in town. But Luke must've been afraid and suspicious. The deputies said they had wrecked their car in the chase. Luke offered them some hot coffee and he brought a fresh potful out onto the porch. I wanted to scream but Abraham had a gun on me. The coffee must've been drugged, because in a little while the deputies were dragged in here, tied up with rope, unconscious. They were tortured and stabbed to death, and I had to watch, but most of the time I shut my eyes. I guess I babbled and raved and pounded my bare fists on the cage." Gwen held up her hands, which were bruised and swollen and scraped raw.

"Oh, God!" Nancy moaned. "Why? Why is all this happening?"

"There's no reason for it," Gwen said soberly. "I keep remembering my grandfather telling me to never forget man is capable of the worst imaginable acts of cruelty. He was in a Nazi concentration camp during World War Two. But at least that was wartime. What excuse is there for what's happening to us now?"

Nancy was silent, coming face to face with a guilt she had just realized. She and Hank and Tom were partially to blame for the deputies' deaths because the chase never would have happened were it not for the theft of the groceries from the store. Oh, what a lark it had seemed to be. And getting away had been the best part. They had thought themselves so terribly clever, never suspecting that the deputies weren't able to give pursuit anymore because they had wrecked their squad car. As these realizations struck home, silent, remorseful tears rolled down Nancy's cheeks. "Damn my stepfather," she said suddenly.

Gwen hunched forward, peering through the wire cages, her eyes bright with desperation. "We have to try to escape. We have to try to get out of here. They'll kill us. The whole family is crazy. They think they're vampires or witches or something."

"Shh," Nancy whispered, afraid Gwen was talking so loudly that she'd be overheard.

But Gwen went on, barely lowering her volume. "I've been locked up in this cage for two days. I've heard them talking, planning diabolical things that would send chills up your spine. Their mother is in charge of whatever they're going to do, only I've never seen her. She lives upstairs. She's a witch or they think she is. They're preparing for a Black Mass, an insane ritual of some sort. And you and I and some other poor girl are intended to be human sacrifices."

Nancy didn't want to hear what Gwen was saying. It didn't make sense. It couldn't be happening. It overwhelmed the senses, numbing a person's intellect, a person's physical and emotional resources, till the ability to struggle for survival was lost in a nightmarish vortex of futility and despair. Nancy had sunk back against the rear of her cage. The fight had gone out of her. She was hopelessly disconsolate and almost ready to die. She even felt she probably deserved it because of her guilt over the way the two deputies had died.

"May the Lord have mercy on them," she mumbled under her breath. "And on Hank and Tom."

Pressing her face against the wire mesh of the cage, Gwen whispered insistently, "I tell you, Nancy, we have got to try to get out of here. Don't give up on me, please. If you and I lose hope, we'll be done for. We've got to think our way out of this somehow."

Nancy spoke through her tears. "But what can we do, Gwen? It's useless! Useless in these cages! At least if we were locked up in a room— But this way we don't have a chance of trying to escape." She continued sobbing.

"Look, you've got to pull yourself together," Gwen said. "It's not as hopeless as you think. In the morning Luke and Abraham will unlock the cages to give us food and march us out into the field to go to the toilet. If I get a chance, I'm going to try something."

"You're not going to make a run for it?" Nancy asked, panic-stricken, remembering how Hank and Tom had been gunned down.

"No. Something else. I'll seduce one of the brothers if I can or both of them if I have to. And I'll kill them if they let me get my hands on a gun."

Nancy mulled it over, terrified of the risks. "What can I do?" she asked timidly.

"You'll have to create a diversion and do your part. Be ready to use a club or a rock, whatever you can grab."

"I'm scared, Gwen," Nancy whispered weakly.

"I am, too," said the older girl. "But what else can we do? If you have a better suggestion, I'm willing to listen."

"Maybe somebody will come for us." "Who?"

"Somebody looking for the two deputies."

"We can't count on it. How would they know to look here? Look, Nancy, try to get some sleep. Be strong tomorrow and be brave. They'll try not to kill us if they can help it. We have a value to them. They want us for their crazy rituals and somehow I don't figure we oughta stick around."

Nancy and Gwen wrapped themselves up in the ragged, dirty quilts on the bottoms of their cages. Silently, saying each word with slow, careful enunciation in the privacy of her mind, Nancy prayed till exhaustion overcame her and she dozed, tossing fitfully and crying out once or twice in her sleep.

Gwen lay wide awake, staring up at the white ceiling through wire mesh. The room was brightly lit. Their captors didn't trust leaving them alone in the dark. Gwen tried not to think about her sister Sally, not to dwell on the horrors she had already been through. By an effort of will, she concentrated on her own survival, and in this, her aged grandfather was an inspiration. She recalled much of what he had told her of the Nazi death factories. These experiences, once so terrifying but remote, now had a meaning for her that she never suspected would come to pass. She wanted to be as strong as her grandfather. He had not been saved by prayers, he always maintained, but by his own ingenuity and a hefty measure of good luck. Those who remembered how to pray and nothing else, died. Gwen did not pray. She concentrated on summoning energy and determination within herself for the escape attempt which must be made. It helped to remember how much she had to live for, which was something she had only recently come to realize, and that made it all the more ironic, if she should die, a victim of someone's homicidal whim.

It had taken her a year to begin to get over her divorce. Her ex-husband, Warren, was a metallurgical engineer for Wheeling Steel Corporation. On the job he was capable and effective, plunging headlong and obsessively into challenges and finding solutions that were often cleverly innovative, bordering on genius. He had the respect of his peers, both socially and professionally. This filled him with pride and a deep sense of accomplishment that carried over into his marriage. He felt that his role as husband was totally fulfilled by his being such an outstanding breadwinner. He expected Gwen to cater to him, as he had been catered to and pampered by his mother and his doting spinster aunt through all his growing-up years.

Gwen had married Warren Davis while they were both undergraduates at West Virginia University in Morgantown. She was studying to be an elementary school teacher, and he, of course, was enrolled in the College of Engineering. They both got some monetary support from their parents and both had small academic scholarships, but to make ends meet they had to take out student loans and find summer employment. Gwen looked upon all this as part of the marriage partnership. Her contribution was no less important than Warren's. But almost from the beginning, he seemed to assume certain prerogatives, as if his studying, his education, and his eventual career took automatic precedence over hers. In the early days of love and togetherness, she didn't bother to argue, telling herself she would stand up for her rights later if it became necessary. In the meantime, she did most of the dishes, laundry, and other household chores and worked in her studying around these necessities, while Warren didn't have to contend with them. His grades were better than hers, and everyone knew that engineers made more money than teachers, so she stifled any nagging doubts she may have had and didn't question his assumed dominance.

She got pregnant not long after graduation and that put an end to her attempts to find a teaching position. Her daughter, Amy, was born the following spring. Warren was already working for Wheeling Steel. His drive in that area giving early evidence of becoming obsessive, if Gwen had only noticed the signs. But she was caught up in trying to be a wife and mother, even though, had she been able to admit the truth to herself, she would probably have preferred not to have her first child at this time. It was Warren who had wanted the pregnancy and Gwen relinquished whatever ideas she may have entertained about going to work, earning a salary, and living the relatively care-free lifestyle of a young married woman unencumbered by children.

She loved Amy. That was not the problem. But more and more she began to see Warren as selfish, demanding, and overbearing. His pride in his work and his ability to earn recognition, praise, and advancements, in her eyes, began to take on the unattractive taint of smugness. The more he accomplished, the less he treated her as an equal. When these realizations first dawned on her, she fought against them, tried to submerge them in the rituals of shopping, housekeeping, entertaining friends, and taking care of Amy. Warren was an adequate father, giving his daughter much of his attention when he was home from work, but even this possible virtue became a fault when Gwen started to think her husband's attention to Amy could be his way of avoiding her. Or was she imagining it all? Was this the way married life inevitably turned out? Had she been too immature to take on the burden in the first place?

These self-doubts and dissatisfactions, never discussed openly between Gwen and Warren, festered insidiously and continued to poison their relationship. They said good night more often without making love or even holding each other tenderly. Warmth and cordiality degenerated to politeness. They talked a lot about Amy and the stages of her growing up to avoid talking about themselves. When the divorce finally came, it shocked most of their friends, because outwardly the build-up had made barely a ripple. Inwardly, Gwen was devastated. They had been married six years. Amy was four. After all this time spent in inner turmoil, questioning herself, her motives, her worthiness as a wife, mother, and even as a person, Gwen's self-confidence was totally shattered, yet she had to go on being a mother to Amy and had to make a career and a new life for herself.

About a year ago, after being divorced for seven months, she finally landed a job teaching fifth grade in a small West Virginia town not far from Wheeling. She had been called in to substitute when the regular teacher became sick, had gone on to finish out the term, and because of her excellent work had been rehired in the fall when another vacancy opened up. She had gone into her first day of teaching desperately trying to conceal from the class how scared she was. The first months had continued to be an enormously challenging struggle, till she saw that she could do the job, and, moreover, that she was good at it. The children, resentful at first because she had replaced their original teacher, eventually settled down, did what she told them, and even liked her. A milestone of her comeback from her divorce was the day Johnny Adams, one of the toughest kids in the class, came in to her privately during recess and said he wanted to pass fifth grade but if he failed it would be okay because he'd get to be with her another year rather than with the 'meany' in the next grade. "You mustn't call Ms. Wilkes a 'meany,' she's an excellent teacher," Gwen had said, but she couldn't help smiling over the compliment.

Warren had taken Amy over the Easter vacation so Gwen could spend some time with Sally, her younger sister, who was still in college. They had started out yesterday morning on a pleasant drive and picnic. Because of the new energy and self-confidence she had found, Gwen was able to discuss her marital problems and the divorce openly, even cheerfully, with Sally, and had hoped her sister might profit by her mistakes.

Now Sally was dead. And Gwen knew she had to try to stay alive and get back to Amy. She hoped that some of her grandfather's instincts for survival would have a resurgence in her as powerful as her love for her daughter. Her eyes shut, but even in sleep, she continued to sense the presence of the wire cage enveloping her like a coffin.

CHAPTER 9

Morgan Drey, the young anthropologist who had written *The Appeal of Witchcraft*, concluded his final lecture before Easter vacation to an evening class at New York City College:

"The thing that distinguishes man from the other animals, more than any other thing, is his ability to sublimate. His highly developed intellect can and does override his instincts. This has produced some of his noblest achievements and basest perversions.

The animal called man can be noble or petty, comic, cowardly, pathetic, or brave. He has aspirations which are admirable and some which are despicable. He can be taught or misguided to substitute the penetration of a dagger for the penetration of sex, the mindless unison of a Nazi goosestep for the subtler rhythms of poetry, the fleeting pleasure of orgasm for the deeper joy of sex and love. He is capable of perpetrating the worst cruelties and barbarities imaginable in the name of holy science, holy religion, or holy truth."

Morgan stopped and gazed at the class piercingly, to give his last sentence time to sink in. Then he said, "That's it for today, folks. Class dismissed ten minutes early, as I promised. Happy Easter." He started gathering up his books and papers.

A few class members lingered to ask a question or two, or to wish him a nice holiday. He was the last one to leave the room and by that time he was crushingly lonely. No one was in the corridor and all the classrooms were dark. His solitary footsteps reverberated in the hall.

Coming down the gray stone steps outside the building, he put his hand up and hailed a cab. He meant to tell the driver to take him home but instead, he said, "Washington Square." This was in Greenwich Village, near Cynthia's shop. He paid the cabbie and got out and walked... thinking about the intensely zealous, attractive young girl who had told him she never wanted to see him again. He had been unable to get her out of his mind. He remembered her lovely black hair and the vibrant glow of her black eyes.

The shop was closed, its panes of glass caged in and locked. A sign said: CLOSED FOR EASTER. But Morgan Drey lingered, trying to see if there might be someone inside taking inventory or something. Finally, he went into the bar next door and ordered a beer. Sipping it, he thought about Cynthia. He knew it was foolish of him to be so attracted to her because on a rational level he had come to the conclusion that she was quite possibly mentally disturbed. But there was something about her that drew him like a magnet.

For the first time, ruefully, he admitted that he was infatuated; otherwise, he would heed the warning signs and back off. But he lacked the necessary good sense. His instincts were overriding his intellect. He wanted this girl even though she had all the earmarks of bad trouble.

Still, he might be able to help her. Her mind had been warped when she was younger and he was the right fellow to unwarp it. Even if she got nothing else out of their relationship, that much would put her a bit ahead, wouldn't it?

He tossed down the remainder of his draft beer and gave the bartender his order for another.

Those services Cynthia had spoken of were supposed to take place over Easter. Morgan knew so little about her that he remembered just about every scrap of information she had let drop. He recalled the name of a town she lived near: Cherry Hill. Rather than moping around over the long weekend, he could get himself a roadmap and drive there with his camera, telling her he had come to ask her to let him photograph the services. If she became enraged and turned him away, well, that would be the end of it. He'd turn around and drive home, swallowing his mortification. But if she accepted him and let him stay...

What in the world had come over him, for God's sakes? He was coming on like a love-sick adolescent hanging around the schoolyard for a glimpse of his secret heartthrob. He was certainly not comporting himself like a dignified twenty-eight-year-old anthropologist.

Tonight he'd get drunk and in the morning the hangover might discourage him from going to Cherry Hill and making a fool of himself. In a wry frame of mind, he ordered a double shot of whisky to go with his third draft.

CHAPTER 10

Nancy awoke at four in the morning and could not sleep anymore. Gwen's supposedly upcoming escape attempt both tormented and tantalized her. If it only worked. But it wouldn't. Then, again, it might. Locked inside the wire cage, Nancy couldn't picture herself free. The images had no tangibility. She had to fight against giving up. Her mind was mostly a blank. Her life wasn't passing in front of her. Maybe that meant she wasn't going to die.

Gwen was going to try to seduce the brothers, Luke and Abraham. Would such a thing be a mortal sin? If so, it would be on Gwen's soul, not Nancy's, yet Nancy would benefit from it; she hoped. It made her feel guilty when she contemplated some of the saints her catechism classes taught her to revere; the ones who had allowed themselves to be butchered rather than giving in to sexual intercourse.

She had made a good confession, finally, after two years. She was in a state of grace almost, providing stealing the groceries could be thought of as a venial sin. Maybe God had inspired her to get ready and purify her soul. But maybe she was still scared to die, even knowing she would go to heaven. She tried to think positively as Gwen had urged but in the confines of the cage, this was difficult. Wild, panicky thoughts kept tumbling through her mind. Either the situation was truly hopeless or else the numbness of fear made it seem so. Not one idea conducive to escape occurred to her.

Her ears perked up as she heard someone's footsteps on the stairs. Cynthia came into the living room and stopped in front of Nancy's cage, casually reaching out and resting her hand on the wire. Nancy's eyes widened. Cynthia was wearing a pink satin robe and appeared fresh and well-rested as if nothing disturbing was going on. She even smiled and then said, "Good morning."

"Good morning," Nancy replied, her voice breaking to a tiny croak as the automatic response issued from the depths of her conditioning, shaking her with a small shock wave of irony and dismay.

"Breakfast will be ready soon," said Cynthia quite pleasantly. With that, she strode through the dining room and into the kitchen and began banging pots and pans.

Gwen's sudden whisper startled Nancy. "Fucking bitch!" Gwen said under her breath.

"I didn't know you were awake," Nancy whispered back.

"In a little while you'll smell eggs, toast, and coffee," said Gwen. "But we won't get any. Luke, Cyrus, and Abraham will come down and they'll all have a nice hearty breakfast and a friendly chat. When they're done they'll give us some bread and cheese. Then they'll let us out to do our business. That's when our big chance will come. I was afraid to try it yesterday on my own. But now I have you to help. One of us might get away or both of us, if we're lucky."

"I'm still scared," Nancy said. "I'm not sure what to do."

Gwen eyed her shrewdly, trying to instill confidence. "When the right moment comes, don't hesitate, make your move. Grab a stick or a rock. If you could play up to one of the brothers beforehand, that would double our chances of gettin' hold of the gun."

"I don't think I could stand to have them touch me," Nancy said.

"You're gonna to wait until they do worse?" Gwen challenged.

The three brothers clomped down the stairs. Luke and Abraham went directly into the dining room but Cyrus lingered around the cages, leering and giggling and jabbing with his fingers, poking the girls from one side to another in their wire cells. Luckily, he didn't have his knife.

"Cyrus!" Cynthia called. "You come in and eat while it's hot."

He gave a few final pokes, gleefully waddling around the side of Nancy's cage on his way into the dining room where he dragged a chair across the carpet and sat down.

"Hotcakes instead of eggs today," Gwen said in a whisper. "How could anything that black-haired bitch touches smell so good?" Cursing was her way of boosting her courage.

Nancy lay flat on her back, staring up through wire mesh, trying to get over the stomach-churning anxiety of the recent torment from Cyrus. Turning toward

Gwen, she asked, "Do they ever let the dumb one have the keys?"

"No, I'm afraid not. Why?"

"I guess he'd be the easiest one to trick."

"You know it and they know it," Gwen said.

A lively conversation ensued around the breakfast table. Nancy and Gwen could hear everything but could not see the participants because of the placement of their cages. They had to peer through the dining room archway on a sharp angle, the view further obstructed by their lowness to the floor and the intervening aspects of large pieces of furniture. Cynthia was giving instructions. When she spoke the three brothers listened.

"When you're done with the two in there, Luke and Abraham, you go on out and fetch a third one to keep them company. Mama expects there to be three. Cyrus, you needn't go along. You have your work to do, sweeping up the chapel and polishing the pews. Don't dawdle about it. People will be coming in tomorrow and expecting the usual thorough preparations. Most of them will be checked into motels in town. A few will stay here at the house. We've got to be congenial and accommodating at all times, just like Mama said."

"She wasn't mad at me last night," Luke said. "What happened with that other girl wasn't none of our fault."

"Be that as it may," said Cynthia, "we have got to have three, come hell or high water, tomorrow."

There was a racket of chairs being pushed back from the table and then Luke and Abraham came into the living room. Cyrus pushed in behind them but Cynthia yelled for him to go on out the back door with his broom and get to work sweeping the chapel. Luke and Abraham both had the pistols they had taken from the deputies. Taking a ring of keys out of his pocket, Luke said, "Goin' to take you out in the field now to relieve yourselves. Don't want you lettin' go in here. Afterward, we'll lock you up again with somethin' to eat and drink. Behave yourselves now or you don't have nothin' at all to eat."

"Why can't we go to the bathroom in here?" asked Nancy.

Gwen flashed a look at Nancy to tell her to shut up. If they didn't get outside, how were they ever going to escape?

"We ain't lettin' you into our bathroom where there's stuff like glass and razor blades," said Luke. "You might get feisty or you might try to slash your wrists." He unlocked the padlocks on the dog cages and let Nancy and Gwen out, keeping his pistol trained on them. Abraham backed him up, both brothers warily alert, not about to lose their captives and take flack from Cynthia and Mama.

Nancy and Gwen unbent slowly and stiffly, massaging and stretching their cramped muscles.

"Get a move on!" Abraham snapped. "This way. Out the back door."

Prodded in the back with the guns, Nancy and Gwen marched through the dining room with scraps of food still on the table, out through the large country kitchen, and down off the back porch. Gwen looked at Nancy out of the corners of her eyes, signaling; be brave and our chance will come.

It was a crisp spring morning with dew still on the grass. The two girls shivered and got goosebumps; they were wearing their underwear and nothing else. Barefoot, they stepped gingerly through the cold, wet grass. They were headed toward an outhouse adjacent to the cemetery and chapel across the field. The thought that Cyrus was out there filled Nancy with trepidation. "Where are we going?" she asked, playing dumb.

"Make any difference to you?" Abraham countered snidely.

"You can do your business right here where we can watch," said Luke, snickering.

"I can show you a better way to get some kicks," Gwen told the two brothers, stopping in her tracks and turning to face them seductively. "Why don't you let me and Nancy take the two of you out into the woods for a while? Cynthia doesn't have to find out about it."

Luke chuckled derisively but Abraham seemed interested. "If they already ain't virgins, what difference could it make?" he suggested to his brother.

"It's a trick," said Luke.

"But you both have guns," Gwen argued. "How could we get away with anything? Nancy and I talked about it last night, and we figured that if we were really nice to you, maybe you'd be nice to us."

"Maybe we should, at that," said Abraham shrewdly. "Why don't we have us some fun, Luke?

Then we'll see if there's a way of helping the two girls."

"Well... maybe," Luke debated. His lusts were getting the better of him. He told himself that the risk would be minimal if the girls were willing to have sex in return for possible favors. Of course, the favors wouldn't ever be forthcoming, but they wouldn't have to know. It would be nice doing it with a pretty girl who was putting her all into it for a change, not having to be forced. "If you were real nice to us, maybe we'd let you go and capture two more," he said slyly.

Nancy was panicked. The way Gwen had talked, Nancy and Gwen both would have to give in to Luke and Abraham or at least lead them on. What if it got out of control and they never escaped at all? Or what if they were let loose and two other girls took their place? That would be a mortal sin for sure. Letting someone else die to save your own hide.

"I've got my mind made up to show you the best time you ever had," Gwen purred breathily, unsnapping her bra.

Abraham and Luke ogled her large, firm breasts. Following her lead, as if in a trance, Nancy took off her bra, too. The two brothers' eyes gleamed lecherously, darting back and forth, taking in first one girl, then the other. It was easy to believe that Nancy's wide-eyed stare was one of desire.

"Over there behind the trees," Luke said, gesturing with his gun. He had turned briefly, glancing over his shoulder, and when he turned back he was jolted by the sight of Abraham already fondling Gwen's breasts, his revolver stuck carelessly in his belt.

Luke felt he was moving in slow motion as Gwen reached for the butt of Abraham's gun but he got to her in time and smacked it out of her hand. Nancy saw it fall. Paralyzed for an instant, she was too late diving for it on the grass. Luke kicked it away, then gave her a savage chop behind the neck that sent her sprawling, nearly unconscious. By that time Abraham had recovered and was repeatedly slapping Gwen, beating her with his fists on her face and breasts, then punching her in the stomach, sending her writhing to the earth. She stayed down, moaning in pain, and Luke kicked her in the ribs. He picked up Abraham's pistol and handed it back.

"Filthy teases!" Luke snapped. "Tried to make blasted fools out of us, didn't they?"

Luke and Abraham dragged Nancy and Gwen to their feet and pushed them behind a clump of bushes and waited while they relieved themselves, then marched them back into the house, shoved them down into their cages, and locked them up. "Nothin' to eat for you now!" Luke barked before stomping away. "They tried to escape," he told Cynthia, who was in the dining room cleaning up.

Gwen and Nancy lay on the bottoms of their cages in pain and despair. Their escape attempt had failed miserably and it was not likely they'd get another chance.

Out in the dining room, Cynthia was saying, "Tomorrow you can take them down to the chapel, Luke. In the evening you'll be building a fire in there and it will be warm enough so they won't die of pneumonia. Locked up in the chapel, they'll be hard put to give us any more trouble."

"I was under the impression you wanted only one down there at a time during the services, and only the one we're working with, at that," said Abraham.

"Put them in Uncle Sal's office," Cynthia instructed. "That way they won't see anything that's going on till we want them to. You understand; I mean for you to keep them in their cages."

"Yeah, I get the picture," growled Luke.

This last part of the discussion killed a ray of hope Gwen had been nurturing through the agony of her injuries. She had thought maybe they'd be locked up in a room, with more freedom of movement, rather than in the escape-proof wire cages. Now, that hope gone, she was overwhelmed by the knifing pain in her rib cage, which felt as if the whole side of her upper torso had been kicked in by Luke's heavy brown boot. More demoralized than ever, she gave in to thinking that maybe she never would see her daughter again.

Sitting back in her cage, wrapped in the ragged, musty blanket, Nancy began reciting a rosary. Luke and Abraham scoffed at her as they went out the front door. She heard them backing the van out of the garage at the side of the house. The garage door shut, a door slammed as one of the brothers hopped into the cab, and the van drove away. Cynthia came into the living room and stared down at the two girls in their cages. To Nancy, she said, "Why do you pray? It will do you no good."

"Don't you believe in God?" Nancy inquired softly, after saying the Amen at the end of a Hail Mary and then taking a deep breath before confronting Cynthia.

Cynthia smiled patronizingly. "You believe that your God is good and merciful, yet He has allowed such bad things to happen to you."

Nancy swallowed hard, her mouth and throat dry. She spoke softly: "We're taught not to question His wisdom. He sent His only begotten Son to earth to suffer and die for our sins. Maybe He is asking me to suffer a little too so that I can be saved."

"Were you such a great and terrible sinner?" Cynthia said, amused.

Nancy lowered her eyes. Wrapped in her blanket and holding her ribs, Gwen gazed in open contempt at Cynthia's face.

"Some of your holy priests, even the ones you call saints, weren't so humbly able to accept pain as you are," Cynthia told Nancy. "Allow me to enlighten you. Have you ever been permitted to read eyewitness accounts of the bloody witch trials carried out in the name of your God? Fascinating, I assure you. For instance, in the 1500s, a certain parish priest was condemned to be tortured until he should admit he had a pact with Satan. The inquisitors were convinced of his guilt merely because he was knowledgeable about some excellent herbal cures and had nursed some badly ill people in his village to total recovery. It was thought in those days that any unusual talent, beauty, or skill had to come from the Devil. In this way, mediocrity and obedience were encouraged while those with exceptional physical or mental attributes were put to death. So they hung the good priest on the rack and pulled his limbs from their sockets and applied the thumbscrews till the blood spurted from the ends of his fingers, striking the wall five feet away, and all the while he kept praying to his God, as you have been doing now. He couldn't believe that this merciful God, who knew his innocence, would not intervene and put an end to his suffering. But no such intervention happened. The heavens did not open up, God did not descend in a ray of light, and the pious priest died horribly; his religious beliefs shattered along with his mind and body at the end when death finally took him. You see, there are times when evil will have its triumph and nothing can change that fact. Evil is more powerful than good. Your God sits indifferently on His celestial throne, entertained by the agonized antics of His subjects, who writhe and jerk like dismembered puppets. Why are you so vain as to imagine He cares a whit about you? Don't you recall that even Jesus, the Son of God, cried out in His final agony on the cross: Why hast Thou forsaken Me?"

Nancy could not answer. Her faith was not shaken by Cynthia's tirade but she could not intellectualize her beliefs, especially not in the face of a challenge from someone who had nothing to lose, whose life was not at stake. The rote memorizations of catechism class were of no use in such an existential argument.

"For now, you will pray mindlessly," Cynthia said. "But in the end, you'll know that your God has forsaken you and I am your master."

"Get out of here, you bitch!" Gwen spat viciously, giving all her energy to impotent hatred. Crying out so vehemently gave her excruciating pain in her ribs.

Cynthia merely laughed and left the room, scornfully turning her back on her victims.

In a little while, Nancy resumed praying her rosary, reciting it from memory, keeping count of the Our Fathers and Hail Marys by imagining herself fingering the beads.

CHAPTER 11

The sign still said Peterson's Country Store, although the place was not run anymore by Mr. Peterson, who had been driven away by grief ten years ago, after the mysterious disappearance of his young son and daughter. Now the owners were a nice elderly couple, Mr. and Mrs. Jamison. They used the few extra dollars they made in the store to supplement their Social Security. Sitting in a squeaky rocking chair behind the counter, Mrs. Jamison looked up from the red wool sweater she was knitting for her husband and watched fifteen-year-old Sharon Kennedy browsing among the aisles.

Sharon was always intrigued by the almost nonsensical variety of goods for sale, which included meat, poultry, cold cuts, and produce; fresh milk, eggs, and butter; dog collars, handkerchiefs, and shotgun shells; rifles, pistols, and handguns; fireworks, baby rattles, toys and games, and handbags; socks and underwear and toothpaste and non-prescription medicines. Just about anything and everything might be found in the country store except sometimes just the thing you wanted.

"Got any Easter egg dye?" Sharon Kennedy called out.

"Let me see, now," said Mrs. Jamison, making the most of the opportunity for conversation, "I believe I saw some just the other day when Mrs. Casper was in with her tribe of young ones. Oh, yes, Sharon, you look right over there on the third shelf, beside the toothpicks."

Delving and pulling out a packet, Sharon asked, "Do you think it's still good?" The package was so faded and old, having been in the store since God knew when, but the price was only twenty cents, which was typical of the sort of bargain that could be had sometimes in the country store if the goods hung around for years and years till just when you needed them.

"Oh, stuff like that never wears out!" exclaimed Mrs. Jamison.

Sharon began reading the directions so she could estimate how many packets she'd need to color eggs for her younger brothers and sisters. They weren't getting baskets this year because Daddy couldn't afford them but at least Sharon could see to it that they each got a couple of Easter eggs. She would do the eggs at night after the younger children had gone to bed so they'd be surprised on Sunday. She intended hiding the packets of dye in her jacket when she went into the house, bringing Daddy the aspirin he wanted for his cold. To buy the eggs and dye, she was using money one of her aunts had sent for her birthday.

"When the hell is she coming out?" Abraham mumbled impatiently under his breath. He and Luke had the van parked out in front of the country store by the gasoline pumps. The store was located at a crossroads several miles from the Barnes' estate.

The elderly Mr. Jamison, in bibbed coveralls and faded plaid shirt, finished pumping gasoline into the van and hung up the nozzle, then took his time screwing the gas cap back on. He hobbled around the side of the vehicle and spoke to Luke, the driver. "Some damn fine weather we're havin', ain't it? Old man winter can stay away for good, for all I care. Cold weather makes my bones ache. This here oughta make a real swell Easter."

"Yep," said Luke.

Chuckling as if a joke had been mutually enjoyed, Jamison said, "She didn't take a full tank. That'll be ten dollars."

Luke already had his wallet open and he handed the old man a ten-dollar bill. "Thank you kindly," said Mr. Jamison. "Have a nice day, now, y'all hear."

"Right, you old fart," said Abraham for Luke's ears only, barely moving his lips.

Luke took his time getting ready to pull out, slowly starting the engine and putting the van into gear. He and his brother watched Mr. Jamison limping toward the store. As the old man held the door open, Sharon stepped out with her bag of purchases.

Jamison smiled, saying, "Bye, now, Sharon. You tell your daddy me and Martha said hello and hope he gets over his cold real soon."

"Thanks, Mr. Jamison. So long."

Sharon walked briskly across the gravel lot, turning left at the crossroads. From the van, Luke and Abraham watched, beguiled by her long brown hair and the youthful stride of her shapely legs and buttocks encased in tight blue jeans.

Luke said, "This is the one, brother. Purty 'nough for ya?"

Abraham grinned lewdly. "Yep. This one's gonna make Mama real happy." In the cab of the van, he leaned forward, tingling with anticipation of the cat-and-mouse game he and his brother would play with the girl before capturing her.

Luke pressed the gas pedal lightly, easing away from the pumps. The van crossed through the intersection, going in the same direction as Sharon and cruising slowly past her as she walked off the berm of the narrow, lonely blacktop road. She stopped, watching the van suspiciously but felt relieved when the vehicle continued past her, going down a slight grade and disappearing around a bend in the distance.

"Thinks she's seen the last of us," Abraham chortled.

Luke found a suitable spot and pulled off to the side of the road. He turned the engine off and both brothers sat very still, watching and waiting for Sharon.

She was always frightened of walking alone, even in the daylight. The house where she lived with her widowed father and four little brothers and sisters was almost three miles from the country store. She was aware of the things that could happen to young girls like herself. The newspapers and TV were always full of stories of brutal rapes and murders. This was incomprehensible to her. It seemed too callous and unreal to believe in, yet she knew it happened, all too often. Her father was always admonishing her to be careful, not to trust anybody, even the boys or the teachers at school. He didn't even like her going to the store by herself but she had done it to fetch him the aspirin.

When she rounded the bend and saw the white van parked less than fifty feet away, she stopped in her tracks. What could they be doing there? There were no houses around and no other vehicles on the road. For an instant, Sharon considered turning around and going back and phoning her father to come get her at the store but that would be silly. He was sick and she shouldn't panic over nothing and make him get up out of bed. The two men in the van didn't seem to be paying her any mind. They were talking about something. Maybe they were lost and were waiting for her so they could ask directions.

She resumed walking, picking up her pace so she could get past this white van as quickly as possible and be less scared. But when she got closer the two men looked up, staring at her, steadfastly watching her approach. They both had disturbing grins on their faces. The looks they gave her were brazen, insulting, as though they were undressing her with their eyes. She lowered her gaze to the ground feeling shrunken and frightened and demure. She clutched the brown bag she was carrying tightly to her breasts and walked in a mincing gait, wanting suddenly to seem as young and immature and unsexy as possible so that maybe these two men would leave her alone.

When she was almost past the van, the horn blared loudly, shaking her so badly that she dropped her bag. She turned, expecting to be attacked, but the engine started up and the van peeled out, screeching and spraying clods of black dirt, and the man on the passenger's side turned around laughing at her as the vehicle sped down the road.

"Darn idiots!" she said aloud to exorcise her fear. She was upset but glad that the men had gone. The sun was bright in a cloudless April sky but that was not the only reason she was perspiring. She stooped and examined the carton of eggs she had been carrying in her bag. Two eggs had broken when the bag hit the asphalt at the side of the road. Smarting from the loss, she removed the good eggs temporarily and scraped the mess from the broken ones out, then wiped her fingers on the grass. In a little while, she had the good eggs back in the carton and the carton back in the bag. She started walking again, hurrying, her trip to the store having become an ordeal.

Her anxiety increased when she approached a stretch where the road was rather thickly wooded on both sides but she had to get past this if she expected to walk the rest of the way home. It was here that Luke and Abraham leaped upon her, punching at her and knocking her to the ground. They had concealed the van in a narrow cul-de-sac some distance away so they could pounce on the girl from cover, on foot. The sudden ferociousness of their attack was overpowering, giving Sharon no chance to fight back or flee. They stood back momentarily, leering at her, taking sadistic enjoyment out of her feeble attempt to crawl away. Eggs were smashed all over the blacktop pavement. Sharon's breath was knocked out of her. She was badly hurt, nearly unconscious, and terrified. Seeing her struggling to crawl on her hands and knees, Abraham lashed out and kicked her in the ribs, sending her sprawling on her face. With excruciating, blinding pain, her right cheekbone smacked and scraped against the pavement. Abraham drew back his boot to kick her again.

"Easy, now!" Luke shouted. "Don't want to kill this one or Mama will have her dander up for sure."

Abraham produced a coil of nylon rope from his hip pocket and he and Luke rolled Sharon over onto her back to get her trussed up. In her delirium, she continued to whimper and moan, reduced to quavering helplessness from the punishment she had taken. The two men tightly bound her wrists and ankles, then they carried her to the waiting van; the rear door wide open, a wire-mesh dog cage inside. Luke and Abraham hoisted Sharon by her wrists and ankles as if she were trussed-up dead meat. Kneeling on the floor of the van, Luke gagged her by tying a large red bandanna over her mouth. Then she was put into her cage and the door was locked. She had no cognizance of this, for she had passed out.

Luke jumped into the cab of the van. Abraham closed the rear door, then hopped into the cab on the passenger's side. The van eased out of the cul-de-sac onto the narrow blacktop road and drove away.

"Should have raped her," Abraham said, the memory of his thwarted desire for Gwen and Nancy still fresh in his mind.

"Nope," Luke squelched. "This one could be a virgin, the kind Mama and Cynthia need."

"What about us?" said Abraham.

Luke didn't answer him but stepped on the gas and sped down the sunlit road.

CHAPTER 12

On Good Friday, Nancy, Gwen, and Sharon were moved out of the Barnes house. In their cages, they were loaded into the van by Luke and Abraham, who then drove the vehicle across the field to the chapel, hoisted the caged girls out one at a time, and carried them into a roomy office that had been partitioned off from the main part of the church. Ten years ago when Uncle Sal used the chapel as his studio, the office was where he relaxed, met with some of his clients, or worked on his ledgers of accounts payable and receivable. Now the former office was crammed full of easels, palettes, and unfinished paintings of bygone Americana. Sal's large mahogany desk and tall black filing cabinets were pushed against one wall. Against another wall, Nancy and Gwen, and Sharon were deposited in their cells of wire mesh. Huffing from exertion, Luke and Abraham went out, slamming the door and locking it behind them.

The girls examined their new surroundings. There was one window in the office, but the cages were too low to the floor for the prisoners to see out, except for a tantalizingly restrictive view of unbudded tree branches and clear blue sky. Since it was getting on toward noon, the sun beat down hard on the tarpaper roof and motes of dust danced in yellow rays slanting through the solitary window. One of the white plaster walls had an outline drawn in chalk where Sal had intended to cut another window. The closed-in air was musty and hot. The three girls fidgeted and perspired, cramped in their cages, trying to find the best way to position themselves so their injuries wouldn't hurt so much. The discomfort of their prison added to their distress.

"What's going to happen to us?" Sharon asked. Like Nancy and Gwen, she had been stripped down to her underwear. Her ribs were bruised ugly shades of blue and yellow and her lower lip was split, caked with blood. Her left eye was black, swollen shut. She had remained unconscious all through the night and now had a frightful headache, which made her worry about the possibility of a concussion or skull fracture.

Gwen felt sorry for Sharon, and Nancy, too, for that matter. "We have to try and get out of here," Gwen said. The change of environment had rekindled in her the desperate hope of a new chance for escape. Maybe there was something the Barnes brothers had overlooked.

"You must be losing your mind," said Nancy. "There's no way."

"We can't give up," Gwen insisted. Her eyes kept moving from side to side and up and down, trying to spot something that could be turned to their advantage. One factor that was against them was time. People had made miraculous escapes from prisons when they had years to dig secret tunnels or file through bars. But how much could be done in a day?

"Why are they keeping us here?" Sharon pleaded.

"They're going to kill us," Gwen said flatly. "That's why we have to escape. They murdered my sister and Nancy's two friends."

"Oh, God!" Sharon cried disbelievingly.

"They're not necessarily going to kill us," Nancy said. "After all, we don't really know what their rituals are like."

"Let me tell you something," Gwen said sternly. "My grandfather survived the Nazi concentration camps. Six million people were put to death, and most of them went passively to the gas chambers, willing to believe the lie that they were only going to take showers. They didn't want to face their deaths, and so they died without trying to resist, making it ridiculously easy for the SS butchers. Cynthia and her brothers mean to kill us after they've had their fun. Don't paralyze your will to survive by deluding yourself otherwise."

"Why is this happening?" cried Sharon, tears streaming down her cheeks from both eyes, even the blackened, swollen one, which had seemed puffed shut enough to lock the tears in.

"Because they're crazy," said Gwen. "No other reason. So try to think of a way out of here."

"God is punishing us," blurted Nancy. Gwen looked at her in amazement.

"Jesus showed us that sins must be paid for in suffering," Nancy said feverishly. "Going to confession seemed hard but it was too easy. I thought my soul was cleansed but a heavier penance was required. I understand that now and I can accept it. I'm not going to be like that priest Cynthia told us about who renounced his faith in the end and went to hell."

"Oh, brother!" exclaimed Gwen. "Listen, Nancy, you probably weren't particularly religious before. Now you've succumbed to despair and you're clutching at anything that can make you believe your suffering has a purpose. It has none. Turning the other cheek won't help you, it will only make it easier for your enemies by blunting your instinct for survival. You're right where they want you, under their power!"

Nancy did not argue. Curled up on the floor of her cage, she turned her face to the wall to avoid further communication with Gwen, as if Gwen's ideas instead of the Barnes family were the enemies that might pollute her soul.

"Even some of the Nazi war criminals condemned at Nuremberg became religious before they were hanged for their atrocities," Gwen stated. "The sudden acquisition of deep faith is a common reaction of all sorts of people under stress. Charles Colson, for example."

"I'm religious too," interjected Sharon, in case God was up there listening. "I'm not an atheist, like you seem to be, Gwen, but I'm not giving up, either. Maybe my daddy will come looking for me or call the sheriff or something. In the meantime, what can we do to help ourselves?"

"I don't know right off," Gwen admitted. "Look around for something in here that might give you an idea. Come on, Nancy, help out. I want to see my daughter Amy again. And your mother still loves you, doesn't she, despite your stepfather?"

But Nancy didn't respond. She had started praying another rosary, and rather than answering Gwen, she kept praying doggedly without moving her lips, saying the words to herself. The repetition of the familiar prayers almost took her mind off the feeling that she might as well die, anyway, because nobody in this world really cared about her. The shocks of the past few days had broken her spirit.

"Is that a palette knife under the desk chair?" asked Sharon, suddenly perking up.

She and Gwen leaned to one side of their cages and peered out anxiously. Nancy did not stir. "I believe it is," said Sharon, squinting at the knife out of her one good eye. Her cage was the closest one to it.

"Take your bra off," Gwen suggested. Seeing Sharon's puzzlement, she explained: "I'll take mine off, too, and pass it to you. By tying them together, maybe you can fish the knife out from under the chair and pull it close enough to grab it."

Sharon looked doubtful. "How far away is the knife?" she asked. "Looks like four or five feet to me, but my depth perception is not so hot because of my swollen eye."

"You're right," Gwen said dolefully. "About four feet. We'll never reach it without something long and stiff. Still, we may as well try. We've got nothing to lose."

The two girls took off their bras and Gwen managed to pass hers to Sharon, who tied the two together and made a loop at one end. But the gauge of the wire mesh was such that she could only stick her fingers out through the tiny steel bars. This prohibited her from getting enough finger or hand movement to fling the tied-together bras very far. She tried dropping them to the floor outside her cage and then crouching down and blowing hard at them in an attempt to force them out toward the knife. But the cloth material was too heavy, and no matter how hard she blew, it would barely budge. "Darn it!" she cried in exasperation, rocking back on her haunches, out of breath.

"Well, you tried," Gwen said consolingly, still trying to think of some way to make the attempt work.

Just then there was a loud ferocious rapping on the windowpane and Sharon looked up and screamed. Gwen stared, wide-eyed. Cyrus was out there, pressing his red beefy face against the glass, leering and giggling for all he was worth over his delicious eyeful of the nearly naked young girls. They covered themselves hastily with their ragged blankets. Cyrus stayed at the window for a long time, jabbering and pointing and carrying on, his nose and cheeks caked with window dirt he had rubbed away by pressing his face against the pane.

Gwen said, "He can't come in here, I don't think. He probably doesn't have a key."

Cyrus kept staring, spittle drooling from his thick, leering lips.

Nancy kept praying, stifling her terror. Through it all, she hadn't made a move. "He's so creepy," said Sharon, shuddering. She averted her good eye from Cyrus in the hopes that ignoring him would make him go away. Gwen did likewise and eventually, this seemed to work. When they no longer sensed his presence at the window, they turned and looked and saw with relief that he was gone.

Sharon passed Gwen's bra over to her and they both put their garments back on. Silently, they resumed checking out their prison, looking for a way to escape. Every now and then their eyes traveled to the out-of-reach palette knife, just a few feet away on the concrete floor. It was the only glimmer of something usable but it might as well be on the moon. It wasn't much of a weapon, anyway, Sharon told herself ruefully. Gwen never had thought of it as a weapon, though. She figured that if they could get a hold of it somehow, they could maybe jimmy the padlocks on their cages.

Outside, for the next couple of hours, there were sounds of hammering and sawing. Cyrus was hard at work, making three coffins.

CHAPTER 13

On Friday afternoon Morgan Drey drove through Cherry Hill slowly, looking for a place to eat and a place to stay. After a couple of futile stops, he found that the hotels were booked solid and other places of business, including restaurants, were closed from twelve till three, the hours during which Christ was crucified two thousand years ago. This was the Bible Belt. It was only two o'clock. Not many pedestrians were on the streets but Morgan noticed quite a few parked cars with out-of-state license plates. Feeling strangely about it, he realized that Cynthia's prattle about a congregation must have been a basis in reality. The booked-up hotels and out-of-state cars meant that a large number of people had materialized in this out-of-the-way West Virginia hamlet for the services Cynthia had talked about so proudly.

On the outskirts of town, Morgan spotted something called Bob and Dot's Motel, a row of ten plain yellow-brick units in no discernible architectural style, set back off the road in a gravel lot adjacent to Bob and Dot's Bar. There didn't appear to be a motel manager's office, so Morgan assumed that guests registered in the saloon. Six automobiles, four with out-of-state plates, were parked in the lot opposite six of the motel units, so maybe there was a vacancy. Morgan went into the saloon to find out. Glancing at his watch, he saw that he still had an hour to go till he could get a couple of hamburgers and some black coffee unless Bob and Dot were radical enough not to observe Good Friday.

There was nobody in the saloon except the bartender, a grizzled, sour-faced old man in a Mickey Mouse T-shirt, who was hunching over the bar reading a newspaper. He looked up at the wall clock as Morgan walked in. "Can't serve you till three, Mister," he rasped disapprovingly as if Morgan had committed a sacrilege by merely having food on his mind.

"I'd like a room in the motel," Morgan told him placatingly, not looking to get into an argument. "If possible."

The old man snorted. "Why in heaven's name wouldn't it be possible?" he said irritably. "Didn't you see the vacancy sign?" he smacked his hand on the bar belligerently.

"Yes, but that doesn't always mean there is one," said Morgan.

"Ten dollars a night, Mister. Take it or leave it."

"I'll take it," Morgan said. He paid in advance and without a word of thanks was handed a key to unit six. He didn't ask about the possibility of food and coffee later, not wanting to prolong his conversation with the feisty old man. He had noticed a menu of items such as chili, stew, and Southern fried chicken posted above the bar and hoped these things would become available after three.

He parked his car in front of unit six and unlocked the door. Surprisingly, the accommodations weren't bad. The bedroom was clean and there was even a color TV. The bathroom had a glassed-in tub and shower, which was what Morgan was most interested in. After throwing his suitcase on the bed, he got undressed and took a long, hot shower. While the water beat against the nape of his neck, he thought about Cynthia. Now that he was this close to her, his trip to Cherry Hill seemed wildly foolish. Maybe he should get a good night's rest and drive back to New York, keeping it to himself that he had ever been so impetuous. Anybody who found out about this would laugh at him. Cynthia would probably laugh when he encountered her. What did he expect her to do; fall in love with him? Such things only happened in the movies. In real life, these escapades ended in embarrassment and rejection, not in stealing the bride from the altar as Dustin Hoffman did in *The Graduate*. But Morgan knew he would not turn around and go home. Something inside him always made him see each misadventure through to its vainglorious conclusion. As an anthropologist, he was scrupulously logical and rational but his personal life was often ruled by a flamboyant, quixotic streak he had never been able to repress. Sometimes he told himself this was what made him a human being, although a flawed one, rather than a cold, formidable, unapproachable scientist, like several of his more staid colleagues.

Two days ago he had gotten absurdly drunk in the Greenwich Village bar next door to Cynthia's shop and had allowed himself to be picked up by a prostitute, on the theory that it would be good therapy. He had spent the night with her, falling asleep leadenly after a determined effort to blunt his passions and take the edge off his nutty impulse to hop in his car and drive six hundred miles to see Cynthia uninvited. When he awoke in a hotel room, the prostitute was gone and he was badly hungover. But he filled himself up with pancakes and coffee and drove all the way down through Pennsylvania in one day. Last night he had stayed in a hotel in Wheeling, West Virginia, and today he had driven the final two hundred miles to Cherry Hill. He was so tired his nerves were on edge and he couldn't help having some severe trepidations about the outcome of all this. He still didn't know exactly where Cynthia lived. He had checked a telephone directory in one of the filled-up hotels where he had tried to get a room but there was no listing under her last name. His idea was to freshen himself up, get some food into his stomach, and ask around town after three o'clock when the merchants reopened their doors.

Lying on his bed in T-shirt and shorts, he fell asleep watching television, and when he awoke it was almost four o'clock. He got into a sweater and slacks and combed his hair, then crossed the parking lot to the bar and found it lively. He liked the smells of coffee, french fries, and chicken. The old man who had checked him in was nowhere in sight, and a much younger fellow was behind the bar, waiting on half a dozen customers. Several tables and booths were filled too. Country and Western music blared from the jukebox.

Morgan sat on a barstool, purposely sandwiching himself between two men with whom he might be able to strike up a conversation. These men didn't look like Cherry Hill residents; instead, they might be out-of-towners here for Cynthia's services, part of her congregation. If so, they would know how to get to her place.

The bartender, a stocky, bald-headed man in gray work-clothes, took Morgan's order for chicken, French fries, coleslaw, and black coffee. It was more than he wanted to eat but he figured that if he had a substantial meal to linger over it would give him more time to get something going with someone who had the information he was after. In the meantime, trying to be unobtrusive, he checked out the other patrons, who all appeared pretty normal considering the fact that at least some of them were probably indulging in fantasies of witchcraft, sorcery, and related hocus-pocus. Maybe their idiosyncrasies were harmless but Morgan didn't think so. To him, they represented an aberration, a social retrogression that, at best, encouraged neurosis, and at worst led to schizophrenia. It might already be too late to rescue Cynthia from her delusions.

When the bartender brought his meal, he inquired loudly, wanting to be overheard: "Do you happen to know a young lady named Cynthia Barnes?"

"Why?"

The bartender's reply was natural and friendly enough but Morgan had the feeling that conversations at the bar and at nearby tables had come to a halt. "I'm trying to get to her house," he said, keeping his volume up.

"There's not a Barnes family in town that I can think of," said the bartender. "Seems like there ought to be; it's a common enough name. But there ain't. If there was, I'd know about it. Not much escapes a fellow's attention in a town this small."

"How about in some of the outlying areas?"

"Could be, but I'm afraid I can't tell you for sure. Like me to freshen your coffee?"

Morgan nodded his head and the bartender poured from a full, steaming pot. The level of conversation in the place didn't quite seem to return to normal. It was hard for him to believe that his questions could have been this unsettling. Maybe it was his imagination. He was too keyed up to trust his perceptions. He spread butter on a hot home-baked roll and took a bite of it along with a forkful of delicious fried chicken.

"Pardon me, sir," the man on the barstool to his right said. "May I ask how you've come to know Cynthia Barnes?"

Turning, Morgan saw a slender little man with a handsome, weathered face, neat gray mustache, and slickly parted and combed gray hair worn just long enough to touch the tops of his ears. He was in white shoes, slacks, and shirt, with a powder-blue sport jacket, a gold bracelet on one wrist, a gold watch on the other. His clothes were stylish and expensive-looking. He looked like an actor or a doctor, or an actor who might play a doctor on television. Morgan noticed his ring with an emblem of a skull, the eyes set with tiny rubies.

"I knew Cynthia in New York," Morgan said. "We dated, got to know each other, and she told me about some goings-on down here. She invited me to come."

"How is it you don't have her address?" The man wore a smile but there was no humor in his question. The gentleman next to him was hunched forward on his stool, peering around him to scrutinize Morgan.

It seemed best to continue lying, now that he had already lied about being invited. "She gave me her address before she closed her store in Greenwich Village for the Easter holidays. I have no idea how I lost it and she doesn't have a listed phone but I drove down here anyway. I didn't want to miss out on the things she described."

"You've been in the store?"

"Many times."

The man smiled. "Did you ever buy a witch's bottle?" he asked, giving the strange question an air of flippancy.

Morgan said, "Cynthia let me photograph some without buying them, for a book I was writing."

The man mulled this over. Finally, he stuck out his hand. "My name is Harvey Bronson. My friend here is John Logan. We are chiropractors from Columbus, Ohio."

"Morgan Drey. I'm an anthropologist. Pleased to meet you."

John Logan was short and stout, not fat but powerful looking, and as well dressed as Harvey Bronson. Shaking hands with Morgan, Logan said, "I hope you'll forgive us for being careful. Now that we understand you as a friend, we'll be happy to take you out to the Barnes estate with us. It's a pleasant drive, fifteen miles or so out into the countryside."

"If it's that far, I'd rather follow in my own car," said Morgan, thinking that he might have to leave by himself if Cynthia made him feel unwelcome.

"Yes, that would be better," Bronson agreed. He signaled the bartender for another round of cocktails and offered to buy Morgan a drink but Morgan said no, thanks, coffee was all he wanted.

"Hungover?" Logan chortled.

"You guessed it," Morgan said, managing a dry chuckle.

The bartender brought two fresh cocktails and Bronson pulled out a wad of bills.

"Excuse me for a moment," Logan said, then hopped down off his barstool. He crossed the dance floor, in his half-waddling, short-legged gait, to a large circular booth on the far side of the dining area where a group of urbane-seeming men and women were eating and drinking. Morgan's attention remained briefly on Logan while Bronson was preoccupied with paying for the drinks he had ordered. Logan had approached a white-haired patriarchal gentleman, a commanding presence who must've weighed about three hundred pounds and seemed to be in charge of the people in the booth. After a nod of his head acknowledging Logan's presence, the white-haired gentleman remained seated, listening intently while Logan talked to him, apparently imparting information, but they were too far away for Morgan to hear what was being said. When Logan got done talking, the white-haired man replied at some length, his eyes meeting Logan's piercingly, his lip movements clearly defined, as if issuing orders which must not be misunderstood. Morgan could make nothing out from the lip movements.

"Those people in the booth are friends too," Harvey Bronson said. "But you can see that for yourself, Morgan." His eyes twinkled conspiratorially. "The man John is talking to is an extraordinary fellow. A mortician, Stanford Slater, from San Francisco. Perhaps you've heard of him."

"Can't say I have," Morgan said, hoping the admission wasn't a faux pas. Bronson merely sipped his gin-and-tonic noncommittally while Logan waddled back across the dance floor and hopped up onto his stool.

It gave Morgan an eerie feeling to be surrounded by people who thought they were witches. He figured that the American Chiropractic Association would be as dismayed by Logan and Bronson and their dabbling in witchcraft as a group of nuclear physicists would be if one of their kind turned out to be an alchemist.

Morgan finished his chicken and french fries and his last sip of cold coffee. Turning to Bronson, he said, "What time are we leaving?"

"I'm ready now," Bronson said. "How about you, John?"

"Soon as I finish this," said Logan, gesturing with his drink.

Morgan glanced across the dance floor to the booth on the far side and saw that the patriarchal mortician

Stanford Slater and his entourage were on the move, getting up from their table.

"Are they going out to Cynthia's too?" asked Morgan.

"Yes, of course. We all are," Bronson replied cheerfully.

"Quite a crowd," Morgan said, making small talk.

Bronson eyed him appraisingly. "You really find all this a bit silly, don't you?"

It was both a question and an accusation, and Morgan did not know how to take it or what to say.

"Don't worry," said Bronson, smiling suddenly. "Some of the rest of us aren't totally serious about it either but it's fascinating, isn't it? It reminds me of primal-scream therapy; getting all the ugliness out of one's system in one weekend each year. We need outbursts like this, you see, at least some of us do because our modern age requires us to be too rational, dignified, and restrained. Take me, for example. I can't tell you the number of patients I've had to be nice to when I felt like twisting their necks the wrong way."

"I agree, that is fascinating," said Morgan, wondering just how wild things were going to get.

Logan said, "Of course, Cynthia thinks she's the high priestess and we're the followers but really it's us egging her on, pushing her to new and greater excesses. It's something, though, how she's got those brothers of hers totally under her control."

"Some of us don't really believe in all the hocus-pocus," said Bronson. "But Cynthia does. So do most of the others. The rest of us recognize it as an excuse to do what we want to do anyway. It's like a true-blue housewife getting drunk before she screws the milkman."

"I'll bet this weekend is gonna be a corker," Logan enthused, getting up from his stool. "You could feel it in the air. I wouldn't miss it for anything."

"Where's your car, Morgan?" Bronson asked.

"In front of unit six."

"I suggest you check out and plan on staying with us at the house. Cynthia won't mind. Can you be ready in a half-hour?"

Morgan said that he could. Inwardly, he was elated at the invitation to stay at Cynthia's place and heartened by Logan's blithe assurance that Cynthia wouldn't mind. Maybe he had done the right thing in driving down here after all. Even if his romantic aspirations were eventually thwarted, at least he was gathering good material for a book.

Following closely behind Harvey Bronson's silver Cadillac, Morgan Drey pulled into the long gravel driveway of the Barnes estate. Several late-model cars were parked there ahead of him. Slamming the door of his badly rusted green Plymouth, he took in the tree-shrouded view of the house with some surprise, finding it much more elegant than he had imagined, and Cynthia came out onto the front porch. She stood perfectly still, gazing at him in an unresponsive way, not glad to see him, not angry apparently, but lovely and remote in a spotless white hostess gown framed by two white pillars on the wide porch of the mansion. "Hello!" he called out tentatively as if she were a beautiful but forbidden vision that could be frightened away by the sound of his voice.

"Morgan," she said, offering her slender white hand as he came closer; John Logan and Harvey Bronson close behind as he ascended the gray stone steps. Cynthia's hand briefly in Morgan's, he stood at her side in the coolness of evening and realized by a glimpse into the well-lighted living room that she must have known he was coming. Stanford Slater and his entourage were already there and, of course, had passed the word along so that Cynthia wouldn't be taken by surprise.

She shook hands with Logan and Bronson and said, "Do come in. Join the other guests and have some wine and relax."

Hoping it was his imagination, Morgan seemed to sense that she was much warmer toward the two chiropractors than she had been toward him.

Going past her on his way into the house, he let his eyes scan her face for some clue as to his degree of welcome, but she gave no such clue and his spirits sank. He felt that if she truly wanted him there, she'd show it more, unless she was merely going to make him suffer a bit, for having the gall to crash her party. She seemed regal, aloof, in total command of a setting in which she belonged and he did not. She didn't introduce him to anybody either. But a tall, darkly handsome man in a three-piece blue suit came over to him and jauntily handed him a glass of red wine.

"I'm Luke Barnes," the man said, "Cynthia's brother."

"Pleasure to meet you," Morgan said gratefully, shaking hands. "My name is Morgan Drey."

"You're the one who's in love with my sister," Luke said quite loudly, a brazen leer on his handsome but devilish face as if he were an adolescent poking fun at another kid in the schoolyard at recess.

Stuck for a comeback, Morgan almost stammered and Luke's impudent grin erupted into cruel, bucolic laughter. Then Luke pivoted and walked away, leaving Morgan stranded in the middle of the room wondering how many of the guests had overheard Luke's taunting remark. Embarrassed and trying not to show it, he made his way to a straight-backed chair in a corner of the overly crowded living room, with its high beamed ceiling and heavy Victorian furniture. He downed half his wine in a series of rapid gulps, thinking that if he got a little loaded he might relax and enjoy himself and not get his feelings hurt so easily. Bronson and Logan seemed to know everybody at the party and moved about at their ease. Cynthia was carrying on a conversation across the room with the mortician, Stanford Slater, whose huge bulk reposed pontifically in a gigantic armchair upholstered in a gay, flowery pattern. The overall mood and chatter were reminiscent of any ordinary cocktail party, except for an ominous undercurrent Morgan could not quite put his finger on. Again, maybe it was his imagination. He felt an overpowering need to get Cynthia separated from the others somehow so he could talk to her.

Well, being a wallflower wasn't going to help. Making up his mind to socialize, he stood up, quaffed his wine, and took a decisive step or two in the direction of Cynthia Barnes and Stanford Slater who were now surrounded by several others, but he was stopped by Harvey Bronson, who appeared tipsy.

"Isn't this rural environment wonderful!" Bronson exclaimed slurringly.

"Clean air," said Morgan, making himself agreeable.

"No, I don't mean the air," the chiropractor snapped back almost petulantly. "I'm referring to the absence of civilization. You can get away with murder out here. Morgan, allow me to refill your wineglass." He did so, pouring from a crystal decanter that he plucked from a nearby mahogany buffet and then handed the full glass to Morgan before excusing himself and sidestepping toward an attractive but very sober-looking young woman who was now sitting in the straight-backed chair Morgan had vacated.

Morgan stood his ground for a moment, sipping wine and surveying the partyers. He wanted to shake his head in consternation when he thought of the common bond that had drawn them together in this out-of-the-way place, way off the beaten track, in the backwoods of West Virginia. These people who professed to be witches seemed middle-to-upper-class for the most part. Well dressed, fashionable, reasonably educated, they were the sort whose jaded tastes might as easily have run to something like wife-swapping instead of to the kinkiness of witchcraft. Socializing with one another over drinks and cigarettes, they talked of politics, economics, travel, inflation, and so on. They didn't laugh much, though.

And what laughter Morgan heard seemed tinny, forced, artificial, unless it was laughter like Luke's, coming at someone else's expense.

How to rescue Cynthia from this sort of existence?

As if thinking of her had drawn her toward him, he saw her disengaging herself from Stanford Slater and the others and making her way toward him with a smile on her face. He hoped that she had decided to forgive him for crashing her party. He wanted to be alone with her but the best he could ask for in these surroundings was that nobody else would come over and horn in.

"I'm sorry for being rude to you," she told him. "But I didn't invite you here and I have no idea why you came."

"I wanted very much to see you. I had no plans for the holidays and I thought you might let me take some photographs of the services you were so proud of." He grinned, trying his best to win her over.

"Mama would never allow it," she said soberly. "In fact, Morgan, I'm sure Mama would never approve of your being here. You don't believe as we do. Why do you wish to desecrate our ceremonies?"

"Desecrate?" He said, with more sarcasm than he intended.

Her expression went from haughtiness to anger. "Yes, desecrate!" she snapped.

He reached out, touching her arm, but she drew away from him instantly, her black eyes flashing. He fought down an impulse to scold her but he could not hope to get close to her by lashing out, spitefully shattering her make-believe world. The only way to help her was to gain her confidence a little at a time, by pretending to go along with her to some extent and then eventually causing her to question her own beliefs. This did not seem impossible to Morgan. He knew about deprogramming and wished he could accomplish it in his own way with Cynthia.

"I'm sorry," he said diplomatically. "I don't mean to always sound so smug and disapproving. Maybe I'd understand you better if I'd be more open-minded. I'm willing to try, if you'll give me a chance."

"It's not up to me. It's up to Mama," she said, still pouting.

"May I ask your mother's permission to stay and see the services?"

Cynthia thought it over for a long time. "I'll take you up to see her," she said finally.

Morgan allowed himself to be led through the throng of guests in the living room toward a long ascending staircase with a dark, curving banister. Many pairs of eyes watched him and Cynthia beginning to climb the stairs and conversations halted. By the time Morgan and Cynthia reached the carpeted landing, it was as though no party was going on down in the living room. All Morgan heard was the muffled creaking of the floorboards as they climbed the stairs.

Cynthia had her hand on the doorknob and was pushing the door open. "Mama, a gentleman to see you," she said, motioning for Morgan to enter the bedroom.

When he stepped forward, his eyes went wide and he began screaming. This was all the more frightening because he had never screamed before, never had encountered anything to tear that response from him. Simultaneously, he heard Cynthia laughing at him, as her brother Luke had laughed, loudly and maliciously, and her laughter was picked up and amplified by the crowds of people downstairs in the living room.

Meredith Barnes, Cynthia's mother, was dead. She was sitting in her rocking chair by the window, eyes wide open, embalmed. Morgan could not stop screaming. The revelation that Mama was dead was the equivalent of a true glimpse into the hell-ridden depths of Cynthia's insanity.

Footsteps came up the stairs toward Morgan and he choked off the gurgling scream in his throat and pivoted shakily, starting to gag, feeling sickened to the depths of his soul, brushing past Cynthia and the maniacal laughter distorting her face. Morgan would have bolted down the curving staircase and out of the house, out into the night, but he was seized roughly by the strong arms of Luke Barnes, and behind Luke were Abraham and Cyrus. Morgan tried to fight, lashing out wildly, but this only amused the three brothers. They pinned Morgan's arms behind his back and choked him into breathless helplessness while Cynthia continued to laugh shrilly.

The people from downstairs came up into the hallway, bemused looks on all their faces. Stanford Slater, breathing hard and sweating profusely from the effort of mounting the stairs, managed a thick-lipped, flaccid smile as he looked Morgan in the eyes. Morgan realized the embalming had been Slater's work. "You perverted bastard." Without a word, the mortician slapped Morgan hard in the face.

Harvey Bronson and John Logan, the two chiropractors, stood by leeringly, glasses of red wine in their hands. Bronson said boastfully, "I knew he wasn't supposed to be here when he didn't know the code. I asked him if he ever bought a witch's bottle, and I forget what he said but it wasn't the agreed-upon response."

"You see?" said Stanford Slater. "We played along with you and got you here, where you said you wanted to be. Only now you're gonna wish you never poked around where you weren't wanted."

Morgan felt Luke's hot breath on his neck as Luke tightened his full nelson. "Easy, now," Luke said, "and it'll be over painlessly almost before you know it." John Logan, the short, muscular chiropractor, stepped forward. "Put him on the floor, flat on his stomach, and hold him down."

Morgan's legs were kicked out from under him and he fell, landing hard, as Cynthia's three brothers rolled him over and pinned him face down. The breath was knocked out of him and he ached all over but couldn't move. He had so much weight on his arms, legs, and back. The people in the hallway crowded in on him and their hushed murmurs of expectancy were terrifying. With a rush of panic, Morgan wondered: Were they going to kill him? He couldn't see Cynthia; she was blocked from view.

John Logan set his half-empty wineglass on the floor by a banister post and knelt near Morgan's head. Morgan felt the strong, stubby hands of the chiropractor seizing him by the head and the back of the neck, and then his head and neck were twisted with a sharp, violent, agonizing pain that ended abruptly, very abruptly. And for a moment, Morgan gave thanks that the pain was gone because it had been so excruciating that if it had lasted he could not have stood it at all and would certainly have passed out.

By now, he realized, he did not feel anything at all from the neck down. He must be temporarily paralyzed. Luke and Cyrus and Abraham rolled him over onto his back and he saw all the people; Cynthia, Logan, Slater, Bronson, and all the others, staring down at him, grinning. And then he truly panicked, so badly that he lost his mind. Adrenaline pumped through him. His thoughts became a wild, crazy jumble dashing everywhere at once and getting nowhere, while his body remained absolutely inert, like a heavy, useless sack of garbage. Because he knew, even though he didn't want to believe it, that the paralysis caused by the chiropractor was not temporary at all, but final and permanent.

"Now Mama allows you to watch the services," Cynthia told him, in her softest and sweetest voice. "You can have a ringside seat because we'll know you won't run away and tell on us afterward."

Morgan could feel the hot tears rolling down his cheeks but he couldn't feel his arms, his legs, his toes, or his fingers.

CHAPTER 14

Just before sundown, Cyrus and Abraham went across the field to the chapel to start a fire. The main part of the old country church, where the services were to be held, was heated by a large black potbelly stove. A small electric heater was used to take the chill from Uncle Sal's former office, where Sharon, Gwen, and Nancy were being held prisoners.

Abraham was slightly drunk and anxious to get back to the party still in progress at the house. He unlocked the chapel door and Cyrus followed him in, trundling an armload of split wood. Cyrus stood in the doorway leering at the three caged girls as Abraham entered far enough to plug in the electric heater and adjust the dial.

"C'mon, Cyrus, I don't want to stay down here too long," Abraham said, clapping a hand on his brother's shoulder to get him moving out of his way and into the main part of the church with its rows of varnished pews.

"What are they going to do?" Sharon whispered, still shaken by the appearance of Cyrus and Abraham in the chapel.

"Build a fire, it looks like," Gwen whispered back. "At least I hope so. I'm freezing."

Nancy didn't say a word. She wasn't asleep, though; she was too cold and scared to sleep and remained huddled in her blanket, knees drawn up in a fetal position on the floor of her cage. Gwen and Sharon were sitting facing each other, wrapped tightly in their blankets too.

"I'm scared to death of the big dumb one," Sharon said.

The cast-iron door of the potbelly stove creaked on its rusty hinges as Abraham pulled it open. Cyrus dumped his armload of logs onto the hardwood floor and stooped to pick out choice pieces of kindling.

"Put it all in," Abraham said impatiently. "I ain't waitin' for the small stuff to catch. I'll get it all goin' at once with a few good squirts of charcoal lighter."

Abraham had the can of fluid in his hand and used it to saturate the wood that Cyrus obediently piled into the stove. When Abraham struck a wooden match and tossed it in, the whole works flared up into a roaring blaze, bathing the room in bright, flickering orange light. Abraham shifted his weight from one foot to the other, wishing the chore to be over so he could rejoin the party. Cyrus watched the fire contentedly.

Finally, Abraham said, "Cyrus, you stay here and make sure it catches good. The church has got to be good and warm by midnight. If the fire don't catch, come back up to the house and tell me. Otherwise, lock the padlock on the outside door and come on up yourself and have a good time. Can I trust you to do what I told you?"

Cyrus nodded his head with great solemnity, trying his best to look trustworthy.

"Okay," said Abraham. "Now, if you need to ask me for help, do it without letting Luke or Cynthia get wise. Understand me?"

Cyrus nodded his head up and down. Then he gave his attention to the blaze in the stove till his brother Abraham went out the door. When he turned, his eyes gleamed as he thought about the girls in the other room.

Sharon screamed as soon as she saw Cyrus standing in the doorway, his thick lips wet with spittle.

"You get out of here!" Gwen snapped. "Out! Out!"

Cyrus was cowed momentarily, his beefy face slackening indecisively. Then something bright and shiny caught his eye on the floor beneath Uncle Sal's old chair. It was the palette knife. Exactly the kind of toy Cyrus liked. The lure of it was too much for him, and, giggling, he waddled into the room.

Horrified, Gwen and Sharon watched him getting on his fat knees, groping for the knife, grunting his satisfaction as he clutched it in his fat fingers.

"Get up, Nancy! Get up!" Gwen shrieked.

Nancy saw what was happening, scrambled frantically, and cringed in the farthest corner of her wire cage. Cyrus jabbed at her with the palette knife, then moved and jabbed again. Both times Nancy narrowly got out of the way.

Cyrus whirled for a try at Sharon, but the short, stubby blade of the knife spronged off the wires, twisting his wrist and making him scrape his knuckles. The knife fell into Sharon's cage. Cyrus jumped back, sucking on his skinned knuckles. Then he strode forward, moaning in rage and self-pity, and kicked Sharon's cage until she was jarred from one side to the other, banging and scraping against the wire mesh. When he was worn out, huffing for breath,

Cyrus delivered a few last kicks at Nancy and Gwen, making their cages jump. After his tantrum, forgetting about the knife, he waddled out of the office with a pained look in his eyes.

The three girls listened with held breath for fear he might change his mind and return. They heard him slam the chapel door and snap the padlock. In a little while, Gwen regained her composure and said excitedly, "Sharon, we got the knife!"

"Yes, but what good will it do?"

"What do you mean? We can use it to pry open the locks on our cages."

"And then what about the lock outside?"

Gwen sucked in her breath, struggling to keep hope and determination alive. "We have to take one step at a time and we can't give up. If we get out of the cages, we may find a way out of the building. If nothing else, we can rush them next time they open the door."

"All right," said Sharon, whispering hoarsely in her desperation. "All right, I have the knife. I'll give it a try."

"Pray for us, Nancy," Gwen said.

CHAPTER 15

In the office of Sheriff Wayne Cunningham in Cherry Hill, Bert Johnson and the sheriff shook hands. Sitting behind his old, battered wooden desk, Sheriff Cunningham told Bert to have a seat, pointing at a folding chair against the wall. Then he said, "What can I do for you, Mr. Johnson? I understand you're a lawman too."

His voice was high and squeaky with a West Virginia twang. His hand had felt hard and calloused as if his duties as a peace officer didn't prevent him from digging in the ground or pushing a plow. He was a short, wiry, straight-backed man with bushy black eyebrows and a brown mole on his chin, his black hair rumpled and streaked with gray.

"Yep, I'm a lawman," Bert said, glad of being able to establish a common bond. "Sheriff, I'm looking for my stepdaughter, Nancy. She's a runaway, seventeen years old. I'm afraid she might come to harm, and if so it'll be partly my fault. She left home because of a… misunderstanding between the two of us. I want to find her and persuade her to come back. I've promised her mother to try and make things right."

The truth was, Harriet had been unbearable since Nancy's disappearance. Bert had not been able to bring himself to tell his wife the facts about what he had done but Harriet sensed he was somehow to blame and was holding it against him. He was in danger of losing her. In his misery, he entertained hopes of talking sense to Nancy, apologizing to her, even though she had led him on, and getting her to appreciate that it was in her best interest, as well as his, for her to go back to her mother and keep her mouth shut about what had driven her away.

Eyeing Bert, Sheriff Cunningham said, "Maybe you shouldn't blame yourself too much, Mr. Johnson. Lots of teenagers go bad these days and the parents or stepparents ain't always to blame."

Bert shrugged discontentedly, the picture of parental concern.

"What makes you think I can help you?" the sheriff asked. "You're not from this area, are you?"

"We make our home in Lewistown, in southwestern Pennsylvania. The day Nancy left home, three days ago, some buddies of mine in a patrol car saw her hitchhiking. They came around the block to talk to her, find out if everything was okay, but by that time she was being picked up by two young fellows in a white van. The cops in the patrol car got the license number but they didn't follow. There was no reason to, as far as they were concerned."

The sheriff leaned forward, getting interested. "You tryin' to tell me you traced the van here? Lewistown is over two hundred miles away."

"That's right," Bert said. "I ran a check on the vehicle's license number through the state police. It turns out your office has a bulletin out. Some teenagers stole some groceries right here in town.

They were riding in a white van and the license plate tallies."

"How 'bout that," the sheriff said appreciatively. "Good police work, Mr. Johnson."

"Thank you, Sheriff. Unfortunately, Nancy is going to have petty larceny hanging over her, if I do find her. She's never been in any bad trouble before but she's undoubtedly one of the kids you're looking for."

The sheriff pursed his lips and leaned back, making his desk chair squeak. Soberly, he informed Bert, "I hate to tell you but there's a chance she's in much worse trouble."

"Why?"

"That van you mentioned was pursued by two of my deputies and they've dropped from sight. We found their squad car abandoned twenty miles out in the sticks. The radiator was smashed in but we didn't find the deputies. We don't know what happened to 'em. I've got a shortage of men here and the ones I can spare have been out trying to turn up a lead. But it's tough. The backwoods folks don't trust any agent of the law and won't hardly cooperate. Lots of 'em run bootleg whisky or distill it themselves in some of these old falling-down barns or abandoned coal mines. The Feds won't even come in to have a look around 'cause they've had men go in and never be heard from again. That's just what has happened to my two deputies. So far we haven't had a bit of luck tracing them."

"Can I join the search?" Bert asked.

Thoughtfully, the sheriff fingered the mole on his chin. "I can't stop you, I reckon. In fact, I can prob'ly use your help. At least you're a lawman, instead of an inexperienced busybody. But you'd better be damn careful wandering around out in the boondocks by yourself. The only clue I can contribute is to show you on the county map the area where we found the abandoned squad car."

"That's all I can ask for. I appreciate it, Sheriff."

Both men stood up and Bert came over to the map on the wall to have a closer look at where the sheriff was pointing.

CHAPTER 16

Sharon and Gwen had traded the palette knife back and forth for the past two hours, each having a try at jimmying the locks on their cages. The only light they had to work by was the faint illumination given off by the electric heater Abraham had plugged into the wall. Both girls had cut and skinned their fingers several times but the locks wouldn't give.

They had to stop trying when they heard noises outside the church. The door was unlocked and people filed in, filling the pews. From where they were kept prisoners, the girls couldn't see what was happening. Sharon hid the palette knife under her ragged blanket. Gwen peered anxiously into the semi-darkness, trying for a glimpse of something through the doorway, but the angle was so sharp that she could see little. A large group of people was coming into the chapel. Some of them were carrying candles and wearing black, hooded robes. The coughs, whispered conversations, and restrained titters of laughter were reminiscent of any other congregation filing into a church.

Nancy sat up, moving to the rear of her cage, pressing her body backward against the wire mesh. From the depths of her soul, she had the apprehension that something awful was about to happen. Something sinful, revolting, and terrifying.

The congregation settled down. The silence was ominous. Then Luke, Cyrus, and Abraham, wearing black robes, came into the office and unlocked Sharon's cage. "The last shall be first," Abraham said, chortling. Sharon backed away, wild-eyed, clutching the palette knife under her ratty blanket.

"What's she got in her hand?" Luke demanded as Cyrus reached in to pull her out.

She made a stab with the knife, aiming for the meaty part of Cyrus' forearm but missing by inches. The big man jumped back, banging his knuckles on the top of the cage, roaring in pain and anger.

"Look out!" Luke yelled.

Sharon scrambled out of her cage, swishing the knife through the air, trying to carve a path through the three men. Abraham tripped her and she went down, sprawling. Luke smacked her over the head with the butt of his revolver, which he had drawn from beneath his robe. She flattened out, unconscious, and the palette knife dropped from her grasp. Luke picked it up and put it in his pocket. "Who the hell let her get a hold of a knife?" he snapped, glowering straight at Cyrus.

The big man whimpered, sucking his sore knuckles.

"Serves you right," said Abraham. "Don't try to wheedle any pity."

While Nancy and Gwen watched fearfully, Luke and Abraham hauled Sharon limply to her feet and dragged her out to the main part of the church and the waiting congregation. Cyrus waddled behind them, after a mean, accusing glance back at the two girls cringing in their cages.

"What are they going to do to Sharon?" Nancy asked, her voice weak and trembly.

Gwen refrained from saying the awful answer that came immediately to mind. She strained to hear what was going on out in the church. The congregation had hushed. Footsteps and dragging sounds could be heard plainly. There were murmurs of excitement and someone said, "I commend you, Cynthia, on the youthful beauty of our honored guest." The dragging sounds stopped and there were other noises. Titters of laughter and subdued commentary all blurred together. Through the bars of her cage, Gwen looked over at Nancy, whose eyes were wide and glittering like a trapped animal's, her body quivering under her soiled blanket.

From out in the church came Cynthia's high, keening voice: "Lucifer, we ask you to accept the sacrifice of this child we now offer to you in return for your blessings. Bless our deeds that we perform in your almighty name. Consecrate the blood we offer you, the blood that we drink in holy communion with you, the Lord of hell."

Still trembling violently, Nancy pressed her palms and fingers together till they were white, making a spire pointing upward through the bars of her cage, toward heaven. She began to pray fervently. "Oh, my God, I am heartily sorry for having offended Thee, and I renounce all my sins because I dread the loss of heaven and the pain of hell. But most of all I renounce—"

"Praying's not going to do any good!" Gwen blurted. "Oh! You're as bad as the ones out there!"

Suddenly there came a shattering, blood-curdling scream. The screaming didn't stop but went on and on, rising and falling, reverberating in the small room where Nancy and Gwen were caged. Gwen shuddered, realizing the screams were coming from Sharon. Maybe it would have been better, Gwen thought, if Sharon had never regained consciousness.

Nancy continued praying desperately, her palms pressed tightly together as if they were pressed on her ears, shutting out the screams. "I renounce them because they offend Thee, my Lord, who are all good and deserving of all my love."

The horrible screams kept resounding over and over, making Gwen want to throw up or to hurl herself against the bars of her cage. She stuck her fingers in her ears but it didn't help. If it kept up, she thought she'd go mad. When she unplugged her ears, once again she heard Cynthia's rantingly shrill voice carrying over Sharon's weakening screams: "Oh, mighty Lord Satan, we worship you with all our hearts and humbly submit to your desires and commandments. We believe with everlasting conviction that you are our creator, our benefactor, our lord and master…"

Nancy raised her voice trying to drown out Cynthia, trying to counteract one kind of prayer with another. "Our Father who art in heaven, hallowed be Thy Name. Thy kingdom come, Thy will be done, on earth as it is in heaven…"

Sharon's screams weakened still more and became dry, husky moans. She had probably ruptured her larynx. Gwen wrapped herself tightly in the dirty blanket in her cage and pressed her body against the wire bars, numbed and horrified, unable to comprehend why some of the people in the congregation would not be moved to mercy and pity. Were they not human? How could they all be such demented lunatics? In the face of such evil, Nancy's prayers seemed futile and pathetic, overwhelmed by Cynthia's depraved incantations: "Lucifer, we ask you to bless her, the source of our communion. May her blood give us strength to do your bidding. Amen."

There was an eerie, expectant silence out in the church that lasted for long moments. Then Sharon emitted one last pitiful scream, lacking in volume, which was cut short and became transformed into a bubbly, gurgling sound. The congregation started moaning and squealing ecstatically while the gurgling continued and finally stopped. From the evil ones out there, a great cry went up, almost a sound of unanimous orgasm.

"Oh, my God!" Gwen wailed. "They've killed her! They've killed her!" She threw herself onto the floor of her cage, sobbing hysterically.

CHAPTER 17

On Saturday morning, Holy Saturday, Bert Johnson drove slowly on a dirt road near the area where Sheriff Cunningham had said the missing deputies had abandoned their squad car. Bert kept glancing left, then right, checking out everything, hoping to be lucky enough to spot the white van or maybe some other clue, if one existed. He didn't really expect his search to yield results. The van was probably long gone from this part of the United States. Why would the kids stick around, especially if they had had something to do with the disappearance of the deputies?

Bert's heart jumped into his throat when he rounded a sharp bend and saw exactly what he did not expect to see; a white van up ahead on a stretch of straight, narrow road, obscured by a cloud of dust. It would probably never turn out to be the right van but Bert stepped on the gas to catch up and have a look at the license plate. Then on second thought, he decided he'd better drop back a little, so as to not panic whoever he was following.

After a couple of miles, the van slowed down, as if the driver was looking for a place to turn off. Bert allowed himself to come up closer; an impatient motorist not wanting to slacken speed. Now he could read the license number and it was the one Sheriff Cunningham had given him. When the van turned off onto a narrow weed-grown road in the surrounding woods, Bert didn't pursue. Instead, he nonchalantly drove past, keeping his eyes straight ahead. He was able to note that there were two men in the cab of the van.

Going slowly over the ruts in what was little more than a cow-path, branches on either side swatting the windshield, Luke said to Abraham, "Was that sucker following us?"

"Naw. I don't think so. Why should he? Let's not be jumpy. Let's finish up and get back."

They came out of the woods into a grassy clearing. Out in the middle of the clearing, Cyrus, in his bibbed coveralls, was just finishing digging a deep grave. The big man grinned when he saw his brothers approaching and used the sleeve of his work-shirt to wipe sweat from his broad forehead.

"Shit!" said Luke. "I told you to have him dig back among the trees, not out in the open."

"I know. I showed him right where to do it. He seems to be gettin' dumber lately, know what I mean?"

"Don't I ever."

"Well, it'll be okay. Nobody comes around here anyhow."

"Maybe we ought to fill it in and go someplace else."

"Naw. That'd take hours."

Having parked his car in a cul-de-sac that offered some concealment, Bert Johnson took his service revolver out of the glove compartment and tucked it in his belt, under his jacket. He got out and began walking, keeping to cover as much as possible, picking his way back toward the place where the van had entered the woods.

Luke and Abraham opened the rear door of the van and lifted out Sharon Kennedy's body, wrapped in a blood-soaked blanket which had been on the floor of her cage. They dumped the corpse into the hole as if disposing of garbage and Cyrus began shoveling in dirt.

Bert Johnson watched, hiding at the edge of the clearing. He saw the two who had arrived in the van take spades from the back of the vehicle and help with the shoveling. In a while, the grave was filled in. The men covered the evidence of their work with leaves and brush, taking their time, doing a thorough job. When they finally piled into the van and the engine started up, from the distance away that Bert was hiding he could hardly make out where the ground had been disturbed.

He stayed hidden, gripping his revolver as he watched the van drive off. He wondered who had been buried. One thing that occurred to Bert was; if it was Nancy, she'd never be coming home to cause him any further trouble with Harriet.

Creeping out of his hiding place, he stayed close enough to the departing van to make it out through the trees. When it humped onto the dirt road, it turned left, headed back in the direction it had come from. Bert walked back to his car and got in, pulling out of the cul-de-sac, and drove slowly in pursuit of the van, not wanting to catch up so quickly that he got himself spotted. When he rounded a bend obscured by trees, he just caught a glimpse of the van making a right turn. So he crept up and made the right also.

There was the van, about a quarter-mile ahead on a straightaway, making an abrupt left. Bert took a chance and picked up some speed, figuring to make the left too, but when he got there he saw that it was a gravel driveway and the van was just pulling into a garage; several late-model cars parked to one side. Adjacent to the garage was a large red-brick house with white pillars. Startled to have come upon the place like that, Bert made a snap decision to just cruise on by, hoping he didn't call undue attention to himself.

Several hundred yards down the road, he pulled over and waited for a good long while, the engine idling and his pistol in his hand in case somebody came after him. Nobody came. He turned the ignition off and got out, looking all around. Then he made his way back toward the house with the white pillars, keeping to the cover of woods on the left side of the road. When he got within viewing distance, he hid in a clump of weeds and peered out. The three grave-diggers had come out of the garage and were talking; near enough for Bert to hear.

"I think we oughta get rid of the van," Luke said. "It could be somebody will eventually come lookin' for the owners."

"Tomorrow," said Abraham. "We'll drive it a good ways off and ditch it. Strip it and set it on fire."

Luke clapped Cyrus on his brawny shoulder. "You can come and watch, brother," Luke said merrily. "You'd get a kick out of that, wouldn't you?"

"Fire," Cyrus said, grinning.

"You two get on in the house and see if Cynthia needs anything," Luke ordered. "I'm goin' over to the chapel to make sure the two girls are comfy and not up to any tricks. That incident with the palette knife wasn't a damn bit funny."

"It wasn't my fault," Abraham said. "Let me go with ya to help ya fool with the girls."

"I ain't gonna be foolin' with 'em," Luke snapped. "Get in the house like I told you. Both of you. Pronto!"

"Aw, shit, Luke, you always get to have all the fun," Abraham grumped, but he and Cyrus got moving while Luke glowered after them, making sure they obeyed. They went into the house, slamming the door.

Bert stayed in his hiding place, watching Luke cut between the house and the garage. He appeared to be headed toward some kind of church out back, about a hundred yards away, across a freshly mowed field. Bert waited till Luke unlocked the door and went inside. Then he skirted along the edge of the road, keeping to cover till he could cross out of sight of the house. Then, circling wide of the route Luke had taken, he cut across the field toward the church. He came up in the back of the church and hid behind a large boulder at the foot of a hillside. It took him a while to catch his breath. Just when he was wondering what his next move should be; should he try to creep up closer to the church or not? he was startled by the sound of a door opening.

Edging his paunchy body around the side of the boulder, gun ready, Bert heard a door slam, followed by a metallic scrape and click. His diagonal view of the church entrance did not enable him to actually see Luke till he had gotten thirty or forty strides out into the field, on his way back. Bert stayed put, waiting for Luke to walk to the house and go in by the back porch.

A light went on, then off, and the rear of the house was dark. It didn't seem as though Luke would come back out. Bert came around the side of the boulder and crept as softly as he could to the back wall of the church, ducking under a window. This was a regular window in the corner while all the rest were stained glass. Bert raised his head slowly and peeked in. He saw Nancy in some kind of cage, talking to another girl who was also caged. Nancy looked gaunt, disheveled, beaten up. So did the other girl. Bert couldn't hear what they were saying. The way their lips were moving, they seemed to be whispering. Could it be they were arguing? The other girl had the last word and then turned away, a wild desperate look about her. Nancy tugged on some kind of ratty blanket she had around her and Bert got a glimpse of her bra strap. When her head turned abruptly in his direction, he ducked out of sight.

He sneaked away from the window, cutting a wide swath around the field, out of sight of the house, till he was able to cross the road again. On his way back to his car, he kept to the woods at the edge of the road, glancing back over his shoulder frequently to make sure no one was coming after him.

He opened the car door and got in, laying his service revolver on the seat right beside him. He was breathing hard and perspirating, badly shaken. His mouth twitched, his hands trembled as he unlocked the glove compartment. He took out a pint of whisky, uncapped it frantically, and swigged down a third of it. He wiped his mouth with the back of his hand, then turned the bottle up and drank again. Laying the bottle on the car seat beside the gun, he turned the key in the ignition, scaring himself by the noise of the engine starting up. He took a long look back in the direction of the place where Nancy and the other girl were imprisoned, then he put the car into gear and drove away.

CHAPTER 18

On Holy Saturday, near midnight, Luke and Abraham came for Gwen. They had their robes on. The rest of the congregation had already filed into the church.

"No! Take me instead!" Nancy pleaded when Luke began unlocking Gwen's cage.

"Nope. Got to save you for Easter," Luke said. "You should feel honored."

"You bastards!" Gwen hissed, fearful and helpless as a wild animal in a wire trap.

"Heh-heh-heh!" Abraham chortled. "Don't give us any trouble now. Come on out of there!"

Gwen scrambled out fast, taking Luke by surprise, tackling his ankles, and bringing him down. He hit hard, grunting his pain, flailing clumsily in his loose-fitting black robe as Gwen got halfway up in a mad dash for the door. Abraham stumbled over Luke but made a diving lunge for Gwen, slashing her naked shoulder with his nails. His fingers momentarily clutched her bra strap but it came unsnapped. Luke yelled for help. Gwen yanked the door open and ran straight into Cyrus, bouncing off his chest. His big heavy right arm came at her in a lumbering roundhouse swat, clubbing her on the ear and batting her sideways so hard that she staggered and fell. Fighting to stay conscious, she tried to crawl but

Cyrus stomped on her spine and ground in the heel of his boot, giggling while she wriggled and screamed.

Abraham and Luke were outside now and so were several other robed figures carrying lighted candles, casting long, eerie shadows into the dark night. Roughly, Abraham and Cyrus yanked Gwen to her feet.

"Back inside!" Luke shouted. "Stinkin' bitch!"

The people with the candles preceded Luke, Gwen, Cyrus, and Abraham into the church, and Abraham slammed the door. Nancy was praying, trying to ignore everything that was going on. Gwen tried feebly to resist as she was dragged past Nancy's cage but Abraham punched her in the stomach, knocking the last remainder of resistance out of her. She sagged limply in the arms of her captors, who dragged her down the center aisle toward the front of the church. Her ears were ringing and she was so dizzy she wanted to throw up. Through her pain and nausea, the congregation filling the pews was an amorphous blur of leering faces and black velvet, unearthly in a haze of incense and flickering candlelight. Her head swam and for a moment she lost consciousness.

When she came to, she raised her head to see Cynthia standing before her, less than two feet away, robed in white. Cynthia's attitude was regal, her features ghostly, her pupils dilated. "Welcome!" she intoned solemnly. "Tonight you shall be our guest of honor." There were excited whispers and murmurs of approval from the congregation.

"You insane bitch!" Gwen said, squeaking it out with all the defiance she could muster. Abraham smacked her in the chest with his open hand, knocking the wind out of her, and as her knees went all rubbery the brothers twisted her around and shoved her down onto a solid wooden chair similar to an electric chair in size and construction. Quickly they encircled her wrists and ankles with leather straps, buckling them tight, and strapped her head back so it was held rigidly upright against a vertical post that was part of the chair, preventing any sort of movement.

"Undress her completely!" Cynthia commanded, and Luke took a knife from under his robe and sliced away Gwen's panties, tearing the tatters of the filmy garment away rudely, leaving her totally naked and vulnerable.

Cynthia stepped aside and Gwen shrieked when she saw she was sitting across from an elderly woman who was dead and mummified. "Meet my mother," said Cynthia.

Gwen once more lost consciousness; she was so weak from the beatings she had taken. Her vision blurred as her eyes went shut. Her body relaxed, her head pulling downward against the leather straps.

Audible spasms of lust stirred among the congregation, under-the-breath sighs and throaty groans of arousal. Beneath their black robes, the witches were nude, coarse folds of fabric teasing their groins and nipples. Some reached hands under their own robes or the robes of others in the pews, to fondle and caress aroused and moistening flesh.

The door of the church opened and Morgan Drey was wheeled in by the two chiropractors, Harvey Bronson and John Logan. Behind them, Stanford

Slater shut the door then followed the procession up the aisle. Morgan was tied with coils of rope to a cushioned chaise longue with a redwood frame. He could feel nothing from the neck down, as Logan, the man who had made him a paraplegic, propelled him helplessly down the aisle of the church by lifting one end of the longue and rolling it along on its wooden wheels.

Luke, Cyrus, Abraham, Cynthia, and their deceased mother were seated around an altar, which was in the shape of a large, five-pointed star. Their faces appeared grotesque, demented, in the wildly flickering candlelight. At each point of the star stood a human skull and each skull supported a tall red candle; bloodlike rivulets of wax running down over the skulls' foreheads and dripping like tears from their eyesockets. The centerpiece of the altar was a huge black-and-red sculpture of an evil-looking goat-god with wild, curving horns and a pair of claw-like hands made to hold a silver dagger and an ornate silver chalice. On the wall behind the altar, above the mummified Mrs. Barnes, was an upside-down crucifix illuminated by candles in silver sconces.

Morgan stared as he was dollied near to the altar and the chiropractor brought him to a halt a few feet away. "A ringside seat like we promised," said Slater.

Rolling his head to one side, Morgan saw the tortured, unconscious girl in the executioner's chair. He felt sorry for her and sorrier for himself. He didn't want to go on living as a cripple. His worst fear now was that maybe they wouldn't kill him. Cynthia's face, her very presence, the mocking memory of his infatuation with her, were nightmarish aspects of the overall nightmare of what had been done to him. He looked up at Cynthia, her perverse beauty looming over him, her lips curled in an evil, triumphant smile.

Suddenly Morgan thought he heard someone praying and he couldn't believe his ears. It was coming from somewhere inside the church: "Our Father who art in heaven, hallowed be Thy name..."

Immediately the congregation began chanting in unison, drowning out the Lord's Prayer, overriding it with Latin or Greek that Morgan didn't understand. Cynthia stood in solemn majesty, lifted the altar's silver chalice in her two hands, and began her own incantation in a high, shrill voice that carried above the congregation's chant.

"Lucifer, we beg you to accept the sacrifice of this child whom we now offer to you so that we may receive your blessings. Bless our deeds that we perform in your almighty name. Consecrate the blood that we have come to offer you, the blood we drink to show our oneness with you, the Lord of hell."

All that Morgan had read and written about witchcraft and its obscenities was no match for what he was experiencing now. Helpless as he was, he wanted to get up and run, fleeing from the mindless chanting and the revolting ugliness of Cynthia's prayer.

"Oh, mighty Lord Satan, we worship you with all our hearts and humbly submit to your desires and commandments. We believe, with everlasting conviction, that you are our creator, our benefactor, our lord and master. We renounce Jehovah, his son

Jesus Christ, and all their works. And we declare to you, Lord Satan, that we have no other wish but to belong to you for all eternity."

The chanting stopped. An air of expectancy filled the church. Once again Morgan heard a girl's voice, praying from somewhere: ". . . hallowed be Thy Name, Thy kingdom come, Thy will be done . . ."

It sounded like a young girl, praying energetically, perhaps being held prisoner. Instead of praying, Morgan thought, why didn't she try to escape? Probably her situation was as utterly hopeless as his. Prayer was all she had left. Her voice rang out in the clear: "Give us this day our daily bread and forgive us our trespasses, as we forgive those who trespass against us."

An uneven trade, thought Morgan. What trespasses could the young girl have committed that could even begin to stack up against what these monsters were going to do to her?

CHAPTER 19

Bert Johnson entered his home by the front door and was greeted in the living room by his wife, Harriet. Bert hung his head, looking tired and defeated. By his demeanor, Harriet knew right away that he had no luck in his search for Nancy, and the hope in her eyes faded.

Bert merely said, "I'm sorry, honey."

"Oh, Bert!" Harriet wailed, throwing herself into his arms, burying her tears on his shoulder.

"I'm afraid she's run away for good," Bert offered. "If she isn't with Terri out in California, or doesn't show up there, I have no idea where to look next."

Harriet clung to him, her face streaked with tears. If she was going to lose Nancy, she didn't want to lose Bert, too. It would be unbearable.

Bert tried to be soothing, holding out hope. "Nancy will be all right, honey. She's old enough to take care of herself after all. You and I did our best to raise her properly. If she runs out of money or gets sick or lonely, she'll come home some night with her tail between her legs, full of apologies, as if that could make up for how much she's hurt us. Then it will be up to us to forgive her and start over."

"Oh, Bert!" Harriet wailed, trembling against him.

CHAPTER 20

As if she had a subconscious awareness that something important was about to happen to her, Gwen suddenly came to, her eyes snapping open, her tear-streaked face contorting in agony as she once again knew where she was and felt the pain of her injuries. She moaned weakly, strapped in the chair. And her eyes flickered as she heard Nancy's distant praying: ". . . and lead us not into temptation, but deliver us from evil . . ."

Luke arose, taking from the altar a pair of crossed human bones and placing them in front of Gwen's throat, as a priest uses crossed candles to bless the throats of Catholics on Ash Wednesday. Gwen screamed, her voice hoarse. Abraham took the silver dagger from the altar and moved in close so that he and Luke flanked Gwen on either side.

The congregation began chanting again, drowning out the distant sound of the Lord's Prayer. Cynthia prayed: "Lucifer, we ask you to bless her, the source of our communion. May her blood give us strength to do your biddin'."

Luke replaced the human bones on the altar. Cynthia handed him the silver chalice. Abraham laid his dagger across Gwen's throat, ready to slice the jugular vein so that Luke could use the chalice to collect her blood. Gwen emitted one last horrible scream, which was cut short by the slicing dagger as her life gurgled out of her and her blood was collected.

For an instant, the Lord's Prayer rang out. "For Thine is the kingdom and the power and the glory . . ." But it was drowned out by great moans of sadistic ecstasy that poured forth from the congregation. They looked on in lurid fascination, overwhelmed by the intensity of Cynthia's services, anxious to see blood spilled again and again.

In her cage Nancy prayed, trying to make herself heard above the din: "May her soul and all the souls of the faithful departed, through the mercy of God, rest in peace. And may perpetual light shine upon her."

At the altar, Gwen was dead and ghostly white, her life drained from her, trickles of blood dripping from her breasts to the floor. Most members of the congregation were sexually aroused. Stanford Slater, the old, obese mortician, had himself climaxed watching Gwen die. In the frenzy of it, many of the witches had stripped off their black robes and were naked in the pews, sweating and breathing hard, anxious to give themselves over to the orgy which would follow.

Unable to control his bladder, Morgan Drey lay in a puddle of urine which he was unable to feel.

Nancy shouted from the confines of her cage. "Forgive them, Father, for they know not what they do!"

Having collected Gwen's blood, Luke handed the chalice to Cynthia, who took it in her hands and held it skyward.

"By this blood, grant our beloved mother eternal life, Lord Satan! So that she, your faithful servant, may dwell among us forever!"

Morgan Drey watched in horror as Cynthia approached the embalmed corpse of Meredith Barnes and put the chalice to the corpse's lips, making her "drink." Blood ran down Meredith's chin.

Morgan looked up at Cynthia as she came toward him, the bloody silver dagger in her hand. "Thank you," he whispered as the dagger came downward, stabbing into him. He couldn't feel it, only heard it punching into his groin, and he knew he must be bleeding, but he wasn't dead. And he wanted to be. I thanked her prematurely, he thought. And then the blade came at him again, flashing from behind Cynthia's demonic face, and still, he didn't die, not till the third time, when she thrust the dagger upward on an angle, through his solar plexus, and into his heart.

Standing over him with the dagger, Cynthia sliced his jugular vein. An approving gasp came from the congregation. They watched the chalice being filled, Cynthia collecting the sacrificial blood. She drank.

Stanford Slater stepped up and took the chalice from her and raised it to his lips. And other witches clamored to drink too, crowding around. Cynthia took off her blood-spattered white robe, her nipples erect, her sex tingling with excitement. Her brothers ogled her sheer, wanton, voluptuous beauty. And then, with Morgan dead and Gwen dead, in the presence of their corpses, the orgy commenced, building to a frenzy.

Locked in her wire cage, enveloped by cries and moans and insane laughter of the witches in the throes of their depraved passions, Nancy prayed from the depths of her soul: "I believe in God, the Father Almighty, Creator of heaven and earth. I will put no false gods before Him…"

Her voice rang out clear and unafraid, imbued with holy conviction. She did not feel the confines of her cage. Death held no terror for her. Her spirit was exulted. Her palms and fingers were pressed tightly together, making a spire that pointed the way toward heaven.

ALSO AVAILABLE
MIDNIGHT – THE MOVIE
FROM BURNING BULB PRODUCTIONS

www.MIDNIGHT.rocks